A DREAM COMES TO PINESDALE

VERDIE EATON

ACKNOWLEDGMENTS

"I am God's workmanship, created in Christ Jesus to do good works, which God prepared in advance for me to do."

To God be the glory and praise for His guidance in the penning of this book; a dream fulfilled.

Many thanks to my family and friends for their encouragement and support.

To the Bishopville Lee County librarians for their assistance; especially Breon

Stephens for his "technical savvy" that helped to make my journey smooth and enjoyable.

Special thanks to Alonda Brooks, publisher (I Am BecomingPublishing) A multitude of thanks for your skill, patience and understanding. For booking and to stay up to date on new releases go

to www.verdieeaton.info.

CHAPTER ONE

Kensington Estate
Pinesdale, Montana
1897

A heated discussion about current events erupted around the dinner table as Doctor Falcon Kensington cast a thoughtful glance at his four brothers.

Whenever he became nervous, he would manipulate long, brown fingers through his thick, black waves. Falcon was about to reveal information that would impact their lives. Taking a deep breath, he interrupted the conversation.

"I have a sister!" he blurted.

"A sister!" The Kensington brothers echoed in unison. All four men gazed wide-eyed at him. Falcon smiled with joyful tears streaming his tanned face.

"For the past twenty-five years, I never stopped hoping and praying that God would unite us. My Lord has fulfilled his timing."

Visions of that day years ago still surfaced in his dreams. He had been a frightened ten-year-old, dazed and bloody, unconscious of his surroundings and wandering, helpless in the woods. It was the grace of God that sent John Kensington and his stepson, Nakai, to his rescue. Otherwise, he would have died. Unable to locate the boy's family, John had adopted him. As time passed, he regained most of his memories.

"How, what, where, and when?" Royce, the youngest brother, straightforward and quick to respond, broke the silence.

"Mr. Ray, my grandparents' lawyer, had read the article in the Pinesdale Gazette about the five Kensington brothers. Given my age and the proximities between cities, he concluded I could be Shadowhawk Davis."

Smiling, Royce said. "I remember." Two well-defined dimples appeared. "The article stated that I was the most sought-after bachelor in the county."

"Thanks for interrupting the conversation with unwanted, exaggerated information," Raven said.

Amused, Nakai glanced across at the grinning Royce with velvet black eyes. "Continue, Falcon. There won't be any more interruptions." As the oldest, Raven brooked no-nonsense.

"Two weeks ago, I received an urgent telegram from Mr. Ray informing me of my grandparents' death; they had succumbed to the fever a week prior, and he had requested me to attend the reading of the will. Last Friday, after I attended the Annual Physicians Conference in Lame Deer, I went to his office, and he presented the documents. I hoped to meet Miliya, my sister, but Mr. Ray, told me she had felt ill and left before my arrival. In one envelope was a letter written by Nana…" He paused, and four pairs of black brows lifted.

"Nana, the childhood name I called my grandmother," Falcon explained. The men nodded in unison. "Her primary concern was that I love and protect Miliya."

He picked up an envelope and spilled the contents onto the table. There were family daguerreotypes and assorted jewelry.

Holding a daguerreotype of a couple and a young boy, about five years old, Dakota asked, Is this your family?" Falcon nodded his head.

"My parents and I."

Fond memories flooded his mind as he considered the faces in the photograph. His mother, Aquabia, had been a beautiful woman. Her dark, almond colored skin and height was inherited from Grandpa Peter. She stood above most of the females in her town. Her gray eyes and wavy amber hair mirrored Nana's father, Sean, an Irishman. Falcon inherited his dark tan skin and impressive height from his Cheyenne father Red Fox and Grandpa Peter.

"Who are these people?" Nakai handed Falcon another daguerreotype. The curious brothers gathered around and peered at the image. A young girl, with a light complexion and long dark blonde braids and about two years of age, sat between an elderly couple on a sofa.

A gasp escaped his lips. The images were of his grandfather, Peter, and grandmother, Zinnie Davis, Nana. Falcon was a progeny from their mixed blood.

"My grandparents and my sister at a young age. I never knew my paternal grandparents."

Nakai straightened up in the chair and stared at Falcon.

"Always remember, though you may not be our biological brother, the bonds of our love are eternal. You are our brother. We would

5

welcome Miliya into our family." Overwhelmed by the outpouring of love and support, the doctor looked around the table at each man and nodded in gratitude.

"So, when will you meet her?" Dakota asked.

"Wednesday. She's arriving on the one o'clock stagecoach from Lame Deer."

"Tomorrow! Good." Nakai boomed. "I'm sure I speak for the rest." He glanced around the table at his brothers. "We're happy about the miracle that has happened in your life."

"Good things come to those who wait," Raven offered.

And God knows he had waited, Falcon thought. He had a loving family, successful career, and tomorrow, he would welcome his sister into his life.

Lame Deer Depot Station

A lovely young woman sat on the wooden bench waiting for the Pinesdale stagecoach. The male passersby admired her almond-hued skin and honey-brown hair secured in a bun at her nape. Two weeks ago, she had attended funeral services for her grandparents, and now she was on her way to Pinesdale to meet her estranged brother. Grandma Nana told her the history of her family when she was eleven years old. Aquabia, her mother, died from childbirth complications. Red Fox, her Cheyenne father, and ten-year-old brother, Shadowhawk, disappeared while traveling to Lame Deer on business. For the next twenty-five years, her grandparents doted on their granddaughter. They instilled in her honesty, respect, independence, and unconditional love.

At the reading of the will, Mr. Ray, her grandparents' lawyer, informed Miliya she had inherited the ranch and livestock. Specifications

from the will state if she located a sibling or her father, she would live with either or both. Miliya shouted for joy when the lawyer announced he had discovered her estranged brother, Shadowhawk, now known as Doctor Falcon Kensington living in Pinesdale, Montana. Fifty miles away from her home!

Overwrought with emotion, she had left the office before his arrival. She prayed he would accept and love her. Her faith and trust were in God.

"Excuse me, Ma'am the voice of the station clerk invaded her thoughts.

"Yes." Miliya looked up at him with eyes the color of a sapphire gem stone. The stylish, royal blue traveling outfit enhanced her coloring.

"The Pinesdale stage has arrived. You are the only passenger."

"Thank you, sir." Her lips curved into a smile. She watched the clerk speak to two men as they loaded her trunk atop the stage. The clerk nodded to an elderly gentleman and pointed in her direction. A short while later, the man approached her, removed his hat, and introduced himself.

"Afternoon Miss, my name is Tom Smith, and I will be your driver for this trip," he revealed a pleasant smile. She took in the sight of the stocky man with kind brown eyes and slivers of gray peppered throughout his hair.

"Please call me Miliya."

"You can call me Tom," he said, "If you don't mind, I'll escort you to the stage."

"Thank you, Tom." He received her extended arm.

Across the bustling street, in front of the saloon, three observant men watched the stagecoach driver open the coach door for the exquisite young woman.

"Purtiest thing I's ever seen!"

"Me too!"

"She's the only passenger! How 'bout that, boys?"

"Member, I's seen her first!"

The other two men glanced at each other and grinned.

CHAPTER 2

Pinesdale Depot Station

"The stage ain't here yet."

Jedediah Pearson spat a wad of tobacco unto the ground, and a thin line of brown spittle settled in the corner of his mobile mouth. The depot clerk was short in stature compared to the Kensington brothers, each of whom exceeded six feet.

Grateful for their moral support, Falcon glanced over his shoulder at his brothers. His sister's safety was foremost on his mind. In the past month, there had been several stagecoach robberies by a group of renegades on the same trail his sister would travel.

"How late, Jedidiah?" Nakai asked, his mouth set in a hard line.

Aware of the worried glances between the five men, the sable skinned man ran his hand over his shiny dome. "I'd say about an hour."

"An hour!" Falcon echoed. He retrieved his timepiece from his jacket pocket.

"It's a fifty-mile ride between Lame Deer and Pinesdale. They should have arrived by now."

"Falcon, don't get anxious," Raven said. Just then a woman's screams coming from the far end of town grabbed their attention. When the men turned in that direction, they saw a man slumped over a horse trotting towards them. Nakai rushed over to the horse, secured the reins, and the animal halted. He pulled the man from the saddle with extreme care. Someone handed him a blanket to prop his head.

Blood soaked the front of his shirt. One could only imagine the extent of his injuries underneath.

"That's Tom Smith, the stagecoach driver," Jedidiah said. "The bandits robbed the coach!"

Falcon felt his chest tighten. Where was his sister? He closed his eyes. God, I know you didn't allow her to come into my life only to take her away from me. I trust in you with all my heart, and I lean not unto my understanding. I know she is alive!

A throng of people had gathered. Spectators pushed and nudged each other to get an unobstructed view of the injured driver.

Carrying his black bag, Doc Jones nuzzled his way through the mass of people. He had faithfully served the Pinesdale community for twenty years, and this week he would retire and relinquish his practice to Falcon.

The doctor knelt beside the man and ripped the already torn shirt in half. Experienced hands moved with deft and swift movements as he examined the gunshot wound in the driver's abdomen.

"He gonna make it, Doc?" Raven inquired.

The man began to moan. His pain-filled eyes lifted.

"Sheriff, make your questions brief," Doc said. "I must get this bullet out of his abdomen, or he'd die. He's lost too much blood."

Raven nodded. He squatted next to the injured man. "What happened?"

"We were five miles out of town, when three men ambushed us." Raven had to lean closer to hear the man's whispered response. Before he could pose another question, Falcon hunkered next to Raven. Worry lines creased his forehead.

"May I?"

Raven moved aside.

"Thank you." Falcon acknowledged his consent. He did not want to overstep his boundaries, but he needed to know the whereabouts of Miliya.

He bent over Tom. "How many passengers?"

"One lady. Miss Miliya. Beautiful. They took her. I Shot one. Tried to stop them." He grunted.

"No more questions," the doctor ordered. "Bring him to my office." Doc Jones snatched his medical bag and headed toward his office. The two men carrying the injured driver followed him.

Raven and Falcon straightened up to their full height. Nakai, Dakota, and Royce joined them.

"I have to find my sister!" Falcon stalked over to his mare tied to the post.

"Brother, wait. We're coming. She is family," Nakai said.

Falcon gave him a curt nod. Raven suggested they backtrack the trail in search of the coach and the missing young woman. He issued instructions to his deputies, and then the brothers rode out of town as though the devil was on their heels. They had traveled about five miles out of Pinesdale when the stagecoach came into view. Miliya's trunk remained strapped intact atop the coach. Jumping from his horse Falcon ran to the coach, yanked the door open, and found only a reticule with the contents strewn across the floor. At a closer glance, he noticed the letter he had sent Miliya.

A quick assessment of the anterior showed no blood trail. He closed his eyes. I know there is nothing hidden that won't be revealed. "Keep her safe Lord!"

The other four men dismounted and began a search of the area. The Kensington tracking skills were well-known throughout the county, partly because they were descendants of Cheyenne warriors and African kings.

"Over here!" Raven shouted after several moments. The brothers strode over to where he stood by a thicket of tall bushes.

"What did you find?" Nakai asked.

"There are horse tracks and boot prints that lead from the stage to behind these bushes." Raven pointed to the deep imprints in the ground. "Those scattered cigarette butts suggest they waited here to ambush the stage."

"Tom shot one man. His wound must not be serious, or we would have seen evidence of blood," Dakota surmised. "It appears someone cut the harness."

"Something doesn't add up." Falcon speculated after studying the area. "Miliya's trunk is still strapped atop the stagecoach and no payroll or gold was scheduled for this trip." His eyes rounded in astonishment! "These men didn't want to rob the stage. They wanted my sister!"

He shook his head in disbelief. "Tom mentioned she was beautiful. Maybe they saw her at the station and rode on ahead, planning to ambush the coach."

"Brother, we will find her. No one harms our family," Nakai said, his eyes intense, his voice lethal.

"They didn't cover their tracks, so we should be able to follow their trail." Dakota stood facing his brothers.

"Let's ride," Nakai said and mounted his horse. Determined

to find, and rescue Miliya; the other Kensington brothers remounted their horses. Saving her was the only thought on their minds as they urged their steeds eastward.

As dusk settled over the peaceful countryside, a canopy of stars lit up the night sky. Miliya Davis sat tied to a tree, her hands bound with rope. Hours ago, three gun-toting men had seized the stagecoach on which she was traveling. Sounds of gunshots still reverberated in her head. Images from earlier events flooded her mind. Closing her eyes, she heard Tom cracking the whip in the air, spurring the horses on as he tried to outrun the men. They apprehended the team and slowed them to a halt. A wiry, small-framed man had approached the stage, opened the door, grabbed her purse, and began searching for valuables. The only thing of value was the letter from Falcon, which had contained the coach ticket.

In hindsight, she had secured her money and her mother's cameo broach in an invisible pocket accessible through the opening in her petticoats' side seams. The kidnapper had thrown the reticule to the floor. He dragged her out of the stage by her sleeve. She had kicked his shin, and he scoffed. "Was that supposed to hurt?"

The man tilted his head and glared at her with one brown eye. The other was covered with a black patch. Suddenly, a shot rang out, and her captor clutched his right shoulder, blood seeping through his fingers. Another gunshot sounded, and the driver grabbed his abdomen and then slumped over on the seat. The slim man called Red had shot the driver. Miliya winced. She said a silent prayer for Tom's life.

Replacing his gun in the holster, Red said, "Help Patch onto your horse. The girl will ride with me."

"I can ride my nag," the injured man mumbled.

"Suit yourself!" Hank snapped.

Earlier, across from the depot station, Patch and his partners had watched a beautiful woman board the stage, and Patch desired her. So did his partners Red and Hank. They may have shared women before, but they'd been "fancy ladies," nothing but loose women. However, this here woman was a lady, and he wasn't gonna share her with his cohorts. She was his!

Hank unhitched the horses from the stage and hollered "Giddy up!" They watched the animals scatter, except one, which hovered near the driver.

"Leave the mare. Must belong to the driver." Red hollered. Hank shook his head and headed back to his horse.

"C'mon woman and get on this horse!"

Red, spindly, and impatient, dismounted his horse. Legs so bowed a train could ride through them carried the leader to the harried woman, yanked her arm, dragged her to the brown roan, and helped her mount.

Miliya prayed. Lord, my trust is in you. I will not fear.

Red hollered, "Let's go!" and kicked his horse into a gallop with Miliya astride. His partners followed closely behind them.

Miliya's eyes opened when the sound of Patch's painful howl broke into her reverie.

"Ouch, that hurts!"

Ignoring Patch's tirade, Hank poured whiskey on the wound.

"Stop your yammering and let me bandage this shoulder."

"Wit' what? Is it clean?" Patch turned his head to look at the dressing.

"For crying out loud, man, the bullet creased your shoulder. You act like a newborn kid. I ripped one of your long johns." Hank snorted in disgust. As he wrapped the injured shoulder, he took extra care not to aggravate the pain. When the task was complete, he lifted the bottle of whiskey to his lip, took a long swig, and then passed it to Patch, who eagerly imbibed the brown liquid.

"Hey, that's nuff!" Red yelled. He grabbed the bottle from the injured man. "Save some for me, and the Miss for later." He took a swig. "Ain't that right, breed?" A malicious grin spread across his face as he crouched down in front of Miliya. He lifted the bottle to her lips.

"Drink, missy, and join the party." The putrid odor of the man's breath made her stomach lurch. The young woman twisted her head. Amber liquid flowed down the front of her royal blue traveling jacket.

"Not ready to have a good time yet?" Red snarled. "Later, you'll be ready or else." The harsh words echoed his evil intent. Red stood up and strolled over to his partners.

"There's a river behind them chokecherry trees. I'm hankering for fried fish. Patch, you come with me. Hank, you stay and watch our guest."

"Take, Hank! I'll stay." Patch glanced over at the woman tied to the tree.

"Yea, sure," Red joked. "So, we can come back to find her gone, and you tied to the tree." Both men laughed heartily. His five-foot-five height and small frame were the brunt of many jokes the two men shared at their partner's expense.

"C'mon and quit dilly-dallying." Red followed the trail into the forest.

"Touch her, and you die!" Patch warned, his brown eye narrowed.

"Ooh, I'm scared." Hank sat down on the boulder. "Look at me!" His hands trembled and his eyes widened. Then he sneered. "Best get going. Don't wanna make the boss mad." His sarcastic laughter followed Patch.

Miliya's position tied to the tree enabled her to see the comings and goings of the men. As soon as Red and Patch left camp, she tested the tightness of the rope. With the constant struggling and twisting, they had loosened enough so that she could free her hands and untie the rope binding her body.

Next, she had to distract Hank. She had an idea. Lord make a way, please!

"Hank," she called in a singsong voice. The gruff-looking man stared in her direction.

"What?"

"I want to have some fun, but only with you." She winked, hoping he'd take the bait.

Hank surged up from the boulder so fast he became dizzy. Miliya giggled. When the spinning stopped, he looked at her like she was a piece of steak. Goodness, was the man drooling?

"Well, Red…" He glanced around the area.

"Red! Are you scared of the man? If you don't want to have fun, I suppose he won't mind my company," she said, suppressing a laugh.

"Hey, I didn't say that." Nervous, Hank looked around, seeing they were alone, stepped over to her, and squat down. His wide grin revealed a missing front tooth and emitted foul breath.

"First, I must freshen up." Miliya declared.

Reaching for her, he protested. "We ain't got time.

"It'll only take a second."

"No!" Hank exclaimed, watching the direction where the two men had entered the woods.

"Please? I smell like liquor. I want to smell good for you." She batted her long lashes.

Licking his lips, he asked, "What can I do?"

"A little way back down the road, I saw a sage plant. Could you get me a few leaves so I can take off my jacket and wipe the leaves over my chest? They will remove the stinky liquor smell."

"I don't—"

"Don't you want me to smell good?" Her lips pursed, she thrust out her chest.

Hank swallowed. "Sure." He rose and headed for his steed. "No!" she cried. "I mean, they might think you're the posse if they hear your horse trotting down the road."

Fear filled his eyes."Oh, you're right."

"Hurry, Hank, before it gets too dark."

Shaking his head, Hank strolled down the dreary road, oblivious of the blue eyes trailing his progress. Thank God her captor wasn't knowledgeable about the uses of sage. She remembered from Nana's lessons on herbs that sage cut up in hot water applied as a wash could eliminate the offensive odor under armpits and the genital area. On clothing, well, that would be as Grandpa Peter used to say, "A plain out lie." Who knew that Nana's herb lessons would not only benefit her cooking but save her life!

Miliya wriggled and struggled with the rope until she could untie the knot and free herself. In foresight, she wrapped the ragged blanket from underneath her, around her shoulders. She needed warmth for the cool night air. Then she removed the cameo pin from the hidden pocket in her skirt and stuck it in a piece of the rope in case Falcon discovered the camp. She headed north through the forest, following a well-trodden path, alongside the river.

An hour later

Stumbling into the campsite, Hank yelled, "Hey lady, I didn't find no sage." He had walked a mile down the road and saw weeds, but no sage plant. He began to think she had tricked him. Then, he glanced towards the tree where the woman had been tied and saw the rope lying on the ground. She had escaped.

Approaching the camp, hauling a bucket of fish with Patch bringing up the rear, Red said, "We gonna eat good, tonight." He looked over to the tree expecting to see the bound woman, but she wasn't there!

"Where is my woman?" Patch demanded. His usual unruffled features flushed with anger.

CHAPTER 3

"Your what?" Red asked, a look of confusion on his face. He also noticed that the woman wasn't there. He threw the fish onto the ground and confronted Hank. "Answer the man! Where is she?" His azure eyes flashed anger.

"I don't… don't know," Hank stuttered. "I had to relieve myself, and when I returned, the woman had disappeared." Hank hoped Red accepted his excuse. When that man was angry, he shoots first then asks questions later. If Hank ever saw that blue-eyed witch again, she'd wish she were dead!

"What you gonna do about it?" Hank tweaked Patch's injured shoulder.

"Do that again, and I'll shoot your hand off!" Patch shoved Hank with his left arm.

"Not if I shoot you first!" Nakai bellowed. He stepped from behind a tree, his gun cocked. Raven, Falcon, Dakota, and Royce appeared from their hiding places, their weapons drawn.

As Red reached for his revolver, Raven fired a bullet so close to the lanky man's face that the heat from the bullet singed his ear.

"All right." Red raised his hands in the air. Hank and Patch followed suit.

"My name is Raven Kensington, sheriff of Pinesdale." He pointed to the silver badge pinned on his jacket lapel. "About five hours ago the stage from Lame Deer was held up."

"So, what." Red scoffed.

Raven ignored the hint of cynicism. "They shot the driver and abducted a young woman. The tracks at the scene led us to you. Where is the woman?"

"Over here, Raven," Royce called. The sheriff strode over to where his brother pointed to the front of a tree.

"What is this?" Raven asked. The sheriff noticed a shiny object embedded in the rope. He bent over and retrieved a cameo pin.

Royce shrugged his shoulders. "It looks like a piece of jewelry.

"Let me see that, Raven." He handed the pin to Falcon. It took a second before his eyes glittered in recollection.

His voice barely a whisper, he said, "My father gave this pin to my mother on her birthday. I was eight." Lord, right now I'm in the flesh, and I want to do bodily harm to these men. I must remember vengeance is yours; you will repay.

"Where is she?" Falcon tried not to sound anxious, but night had fallen, and the danger was around every bush for a woman alone in the wilderness.

"We didn't hold up the stage," Red protested. Wary, he eyed the five men. The Injun was a mean-looking son of a gun.

"You shot the driver. That's attempted murder. Plus, you kidnapped the woman."

20

"The woman is mine," Patch announced. There was a slight movement beside him.

The Indian pulled his knife from the sheath strapped on his thigh.

"Nakai, what are you up to?" Falcon asked in a calm voice. His brother had the patience of a cat. He watched him, knife in hand, stroll over to the short man.

"Dad used to say that his Cheyenne blood overwhelmed his common sense!" Royce said. He ignored the contemptuous look from his oldest brother.

"Where-is-she?" Nakai enunciated each word in a low, demanding voice.

"We left her with him." Red pointed to Hank.

In a blink of an eye, Nakai reached the man and placed the blade on his beefy neck.

"Where?" Nakai growled in a deep, drawn breath. Without warning, the blade nicked Hank's neck and caused a trickle of blood to escape.

"I went to relieve myself, and when I came back, she was not there." The man repeated the identical story he had recounted to his partners. Hank believed the lie himself.

"She must have escaped and left the pin to confirm the fact she was here," Falcon concluded.

"I found female boot tracks leading north," Raven said. "You men are arrested for attempted murder and kidnapping." Raven handcuffed the three spineless men. Patch complained his arm hurt but quieted when Nakai displayed his blade again.

Raven said, "I, Royce and Dakota, will take these characters back to town. Once they're behind bars, we will find you." The men mounted their horses.

Falcon nodded. "Night has fallen. We'll resume the search in the morning."

"All right," Dakota said. Falcon and Nakai watched the six men gallop toward Pinesdale until they disappeared.

After a dinner of chokeberries and pemmican (dried meat grounded fine and mixed with fat and some fruit), they made camp.

Lord, I am at peace because I know you have commanded your angels to protect Miliya so that no harm will happen to her. Falcon closed his eyes and welcomed sweet sleep.

The illumination from the moon lit up the midnight canvas of stars. Goodness, it was cold. Shivering, Miliya wrapped the tattered blanket tighter about her body. Had she not feared exposure of her whereabouts, her chilled body would have been warm and toasty by a fire. The lean-to she had constructed from fallen branches gave her a sense of protection from unwanted hairy guests and shelter from the elements. Grandpa Peter had taught her at an early age how to defend herself with a knife, gun, or whatever was at her disposal, and she could ride a horse better than any man. Many of Lame Deer's finest horsemen had relinquished their possessions and their wages by betting against her in races. Nana, a gentle but stern woman, taught her how to be proficient at needlework, cleaning a house, and cooking, all qualities expected in a dutiful wife. Most of her friends had married and were looking forward to motherhood. She was still waiting for her divine mate, a man who would share her faith and her life with unconditional love, someone who would see her as a valuable gift.

A lone wolf howled in the distance. She huddled farther down into the blanket prayed Falcon would notice the strips of her petticoat tied along the path for him to follow. As she closed her eyes, she knew he would find her. Her body rhythm succumbed to the state of unconsciousness, where desires are visions of reality.

Falcon was coming! She just knew it.

"She's resourceful!"

Falcon glanced over at Nakai. What do you mean?"

The brothers had awakened to the majestic appearance of first light in the morning sky, performed their ablutions at a shallow river, and ate a frugal breakfast of beef jerky before continuing their search.

"I mean, within ten minutes of our search, we found strips of cloth tied to bent branches. Signs for us to follow," Nakai continued.

"Many women wouldn't think of this action and or take the time to." Nakai was impressed with his brother's sister.

"This action reveals her strength and wisdom in the situation," Falcon said in admiration. "Someone taught her survival techniques."

An hour had passed when off in the distance appeared a structure resembling a lean-to, made up of fallen twigs, branches, and leaves. From their positions, they determined underneath was a brown mound. Retrieving his gun from his holster Falcon warned, "Let's proceed with caution. That hump could be a sleeping bear" Nakai nodded and mimicked his brother. Both men secured their steeds to a nearby tree and trod with caution with guns in hand, their senses on alert.

Birds chattered in the trees above, welcoming the dawn. Miliya stirred underneath her blanket and slowly peeked out at her surroundings. She sat up and stretched. The air was brisk.

"This is the day the Lord has made, and I will rejoice and be glad in it. Thank you, God. You protected me and kept me alive. I am grateful!"

Suddenly, she heard a twig break. She crawled out of the blanket and hid behind a thicket of bushes behind the lean-to. Sensations of unease riveted throughout her body. Thoughts of renegades, Indians, or her captors began to assail her mind, but she knew the fear was not God-given. Pulling back the bushes far enough to see, she waited with bated breath.

Within moments, two well-dressed men on horses appeared with guns drawn and stopped a few feet away from her makeshift shelter. Miliya appraised the two gentlemen dressed in dark jackets and pants. Both men were handsome, in good physical shape, and stood six-foot-plus inches in height. She watched as they dismounted their horses.

The shorter of the two men with tan skin and his sharp features appeared to be of mixed parentage. The other man towered over him by two inches or more, and without a doubt, the blood of the "people" ran through his veins. When the men reached the structure, the Indian picked up the blanket and sent a quizzical look over to his friend. They were so close she could see the color of the shorter man's eyes were silver-gray. The Indian's were piercing black and alert.

Miliya closed the opening. Maybe if she would stay still and be silent, they would leave. Then she had a thought. What if one of these men was Falcon? The only picture she had ever seen of him was old and worn and taken when he was about the age of seven.

Lord, should I reveal myself or let them ride out of here? Please tell me what to do!

"Miliya?" A male voice called. "I am Falcon, your brother, Shadowhawk. If you are here, please come out." The voice spoke in a deep, anxious voice.

Her eyes collected tears of joy. Thank you, Father. You have led my brother to me.

She stepped out from behind the bushes, and stood in a stupor a few feet away from them, with tears streaming down her face. Both men stood straight and attentive. Falcon stared in awe at her beauty.

Her traveling suit appeared stained, and the ripped left sleeve showed her slender shoulder. Leaves and twigs nestled in her disheveled waist-length honey brown hair. Her mixed ancestry was evident in her light-colored features.

"Is your name Miliya?" He waited for her response with closed eyes.

"Yes. Nahtataneme, my brother." Her response in the Cheyenne language, their father's people, stunned him. Falcon closed the gap between them and, with strong, arms surrounded her in a warm embrace.

"Naaxaa'eheme, my sister. At last, we are together." His voice cracked with emotion. He looked down into almond-shaped eyes, painted blue. The more he studied her features, recognition set in.

"Are you all right? Those men didn't hurt you?" Miliya blushed under his genuine concern .

"No, I escaped before they could harm me."

Falcon said." Thank God." His eyes bored into hers. "Your eyes are blue like Nana's."

Tears formed in her eyes." Our Nana is gone, brother."

"Yes, but never forgotten." Falcon declared vehemently. "Her last wish was for me to take care of you, and I will." His strong arms again enveloped his sister, who eagerly returned his embrace.

"It's a little chilly. Take my jacket." The siblings glanced over at the dark man who had arrived with her brother.

"Forgive my rudeness, Nakai," Falcon replied. "Miliya, this is my, and now your, oldest brother Nakai Kensington." Pulling back somewhat from Falcon's comforting embrace, she smiled in wonderment at Nakai. She was taller than most women, five feet nine, but this man was a giant, towering over her by four inches or more! Oh my! She walked over to the oldest Kensington brother and gave him an embrace.

"So glad to meet you, brother Nakai."

"My pleasure, Miliya," he replied in a husky voice. "Allow me to place this jacket around your shoulders. There's a nip in the air."

"Thank you," she whispered. The sound of approaching horses captured the attention of the trio. Miliya found herself surrounded by three more men smiling at her.

Dismounting his horse, Royce asked, "Is this my sister?" Raven and Dakota dismounted too. More brothers? The similarities were remarkable.

"Yes, I am. Who might you be?" she asked, sounding bolder than she felt.

"Royce, the youngest and the most handsome." His eyes scrutinized her person. "You are beautiful!" He gave her a bear hug. "Welcome to the family!" Twin dimples indented his cheeks.

"I'm Raven, and this is Dakota," one of the other men said.

Before he said another word, the young woman took the men by surprise and hugged them both. She stepped back, a smile on her tear-streaked face. For several moments, she looked upon each brother before speaking. "How blessed I am that you have accepted me into your family. I offer my sincere gratitude to you."

Falcon again drew her into his arms, and she wept tears of joy. Her sincerity touched the brothers. They would give her love, support, and whatever she needed. She was family, and they knew their lives would never be the same.

CHAPTER 4

Kensington Estate

Nakai held the cup of fragrant coffee in his hand and gazed out the kitchen window toward the guest cabin, located a few feet away from the main house. Yesterday had been a spiritual, event-filled day.

First– Men kidnapped Falcon's estranged sister from the stagecoach on her way to Pinesdale.

Second – Upon her rescue, he discovered she was the alluring vision in his dreams.

Third – She was now his sister!

He took a sip of the black liquid. The way he feels toward her is not like a brother! He shook his head.

Lord, I need an understanding of this situation and wisdom to adhere to your guidance. Did you pluck her from my dreams and place her in front of me? This young woman, with breathtaking blue eyes, flawless almond-toned skin, and honey brown hair. The same woman who had visited me in a recurring dream for the past week. Lord, what is this? She is my adopted brother's sister. Help me to see her like that: a sister!

"What are you staring at with your mouth wide open?" Mama Louise, the woman who had raised him and his brothers since childhood, moseyed over to his side, looked out the window, and gaped at what she saw. A young woman, tall and attractive, wearing a yellow dress exited the guesthouse and moved with a graceful sway down the path towards the main house. The sun-threaded highlights danced throughout the caramel-colored hair pulled back into a ponytail.

"Is that pretty child Falcon's sister?" she exclaimed.

"Yes, her name is Miliya." He turned away from the window and sat at the table. "Our sister, your daughter. Treat her as family." Shuffling the papers in the folder, he berated himself for acting like a pompous fool. The matron lifted a thick brow. She started to reply, but a soft voice interrupted.

"Good morning, Nakai."

"Good morning, Miliya," he answered, his attention on the papers in the folder. Frowning at his rude behavior, the curious woman introduced herself.

"Good morning. My name is Louise Edwards. Call me Mama Louise. I've been the brothers' guardian since they were young boys. Included in that title are housekeeper and cook for the Estate."

"Pleased to meet you, Mama Louise. Call me, Miliya." She offered her hand with a warm smile. Without warning, Louise embraced her in a gentle bear hug.

"Welcome! You are among family." Strong arms squeezed the young woman tighter. Nakai felt sorry for Miliya. When Mama Louise had

you in her grasp, nothing short of a stampede could release the stronghold she had on you. All five brothers had been recipients of back pain from one of the trim, sixty-year-old housekeeper's hugs.

"Mama Louise, please release Miliya. You don't know your strength sometimes." Nakai said, shaking his head. "I recall one incident you hugged me, and the results of your 'hug' lasted a week!" He grimaced. The housekeeper's cheeks darkened with embarrassment and released the young woman.

Mama Louise apologized, "I'm sorry baby, I get emotional and sometimes I don't know my strength. Did I hurt you?"

The deep sigh of relief was clear as Miliya tried to massage her arms. "I'm fine," she responded in a breathless voice.

"Would you like a cup of coffee?"

"Yes. Thank you, Mama Louise."

"Have a seat, and I'll pour you a cup." Miliya sat down across from Nakai and smiled. A rosy flush colored her light complexion.

Nakai looked up at her from beneath hooded eyes. Is she blushing? "Did you sleep well?"

"Yes, I did." She bit her bottom lip.

Why was she so uneasy?

Mama Louise set a cup of coffee in front of Miliya. After adding sugar and cream, she took a sip. "Mmm. Delicious. Thank you, Mama Louise."

The older woman smiled. "My pleasure. Do eggs, bacon, fried potatoes, and biscuits sound appetizing to you?"

"It sure does. I'm famished. Can I help?" Miliya rose.

"No, dear. You sit and relax. Enjoy your 'brother's' company."

Nakai's jaw tensed, but Mama Louise ignored his furrowed brows and piercing black eyes. She meant the innuendo for him in response to his earlier remark to treat her like family. Common sense should have told him that after thirty years as the Kensington Estate matriarch, she was aware of all things involving him and his brothers. Why then did he make such an idiotic remark?

Lord, help me treat Miliya like a sister and not allow the dreams to overwhelm my thoughts. I need to be the older brother she can trust and nothing more!

"Nakai Kensington!" The impatient voice of Mama Louise snapped him back to his surroundings.

"Yes, ma'am," he said, embarrassed to be caught woolgathering. The young woman's smile slipped when he pulled her into his keen, ebon eyes.

"I was asking, for the third time, did you want breakfast?" Mama Louise stood, her arms akimbo.

"Pancakes are fine."

"Pancakes?" Mama Louise shook her head. She prepared the eggs, fried potatoes, bacon and placed the dishes before the eldest Kensington brother.

Nodding, he looked across the table and waited. Louise placed a platter of biscuits with jam and butter on the side and then served Miliya her breakfast. She thanked the smiling woman and bowed her head as Nakai prayed over the food. Then they ate.

"I'll be upstairs if you need me," Louise said.

For the next few moments, the pair ate in silence, each enjoying the well-prepared food. Miliya spoke first.

"Nakai, do you know where Falcon is? We were to have breakfast together."

She watched the long, tapered fingers drum on the table and then frown.

"I'm sorry, Miliya. I forgot to tell you Falcon went to deliver Jessie Brown's third child. He hopes to be back by lunch."

She nodded her head. A hint of a smile graced her lips. "Where do Raven, Dakota, and Royce live?"

"Here on the Estate. They have houses fifteen minutes apart to allow for privacy."

"Oh." Her brown brows rose in awe.

He continued. "Kensington Estate sits on 5,000 widespread acres of land. One day, you will live here in your own house." Nakai noted her non-response.

"Where is everyone now?"

His eyes narrowed in thought. "Royce ate earlier. He's the ranch manager, Dakota is a vet, but I didn't see him this morning, Raven, as you know, is the sheriff, and Falcon is the town doctor. I manage the finances and business for the estate. All four attend meals here whenever their schedules permit." A hint of a smile touched his lips as he whispered, "Mama Louise spoils us with her cooking."

"I must admit she is an excellent cook," Miliya answered through a mouthful of potatoes.

"Sometimes," he continued, "we cook for ourselves." Her eyes widened.

Slightly offended, Nakai said, "You seem surprised."

"Somewhat," she said. "Most men can't boil water."

"Mama Louise taught us to cook and clean. She felt her 'little men' didn't have to depend on anyone to cook or clean for them. We're glad she did."

"Are there any Mrs. Kensington's?"

His shoulders stiffened. "No wives. The others may surrender their freedom for the ball and chain life, not me. I need my freedom." The resonance of his voice thundered.

"One day, a special woman will come into your life…" His icy gaze froze her words in midair.

"I will never marry! Never!" The words exploded from between clenched lips. "Excuse me!" Without another word, he grabbed the ledger, took two long strides, and exited the room.

Miliya shuddered. She sat bewildered by the coldness in his voice and abrupt departure. The rancher could be gracious when he desired, but his dark and fierce demeanor intimidated her. Deep down, there was a part of him immersed in pain. Had she been a woman with no morals, she would have told him where to go, but as a follower of Christ, she would pray for his hurting heart.

"Lord, you are compassionate, patient, and always ready to forgive. Someone has hurt Nakai to the point he is angry and bitter. Help him to forgive whoever has offended him, so he too will be forgiven his wrongs."

Mama Louise studied the young woman's scarlet face. "Don't mind him, child. He's angry but not at you."

I'm hurting for him, Miliya thought. She had winced at the hardness and pain lurking behind his eyes and the cold voice. With a somber expression on her face, the older woman walked over to the counter and poured herself a cup of coffee.

"May I?" Mama Louise smiled and nodded her head of mixed gray towards the chair across from Miliya.

"Please." Miliya returned with a smile of her own.

"I'm sure Nakai will apologize to you once he's calmed down." The housekeeper squeezed her hand. "Of the five brothers, he is the most passionate about his beliefs. He is also bullheaded at times."

"You heard our conversation?" Miliya croaked.

"Yes. I wondered at the excessive loud voice and came down to investigate." She sipped the black brew. "He sounded like a man in a rage. When I heard the word marriage, I knew why. It's a banned subject to him." Louise shook her head. "Such a shame!"

"What is?"

"How that woman hurt him. In two years, his heart hardened with bitterness. It's a shame."

"What woman?" Miliya wondered out loud. What changed him from a reserved man to a raging lunatic?

"Zelia Jensen," Louise spat. "Her parents own the general store in town." The words were spoken with distaste and washed down with a swig of coffee.

"I know I'm new to the family, and you may not feel I'm not entitled to any of the Kensington secrets, but..." The older woman dismissed her words with a wave of her hand.

"Child," Louise leaned forward, "I realize you are a part of this family now, but the one involved should tell this tale of deceit. I can say this: she hurt my boy mighty bad." Unshed tears glistened in her brown eyes. Wiping the moisture, she stood up and placed the empty cup in the sink. A warm smile curved her full lips.

"I will clean the kitchen now. Is there anything more you'd like?"

Aware the conversation had ended, Miliya ascended from the chair.,

"No, thank you. I'll walk around. Maybe I'll run into Royce in the corrals. Have a great day!"

She departed the room under the prolonged scrutiny of the cook.

When angry, do not sin; never let your wrath last until the sun goes down.

The familiar scripture appeared in Nakai's frustrated mind. Miliya's first day at Kensington Estates and she had witnessed his irrational behavior because of one word: marriage. How could he be so rude to Miliya? She must see him less than sane! He would never repeat what happened this morning.

Onyx eyes lifted from the invoices on his desk and stared out the window of his study at the young woman leisurely strolling towards the corrals.

When the chance presented itself, he would apologize to her. It was of the utmost importance that she trust him.

Royce interrupted his thoughts as he watched his brother greet Miliya with a hug. Several men approached the couple, and his brother made introductions. They departed with expressions of

awe at her beauty. Nakai stiffened when Royce took Miliya's arm and led her inside the barn. Disappointment washed over him at the loss of her presence. It appeared his youngest brother had elected himself the blue-eyed woman's champion.

Nakai turned from the window and sat on the plush leather chair at his desk. Ever since Miliya walked into his life, the recurring dreams had ceased. He didn't know if it was God's plan at work, but he did know last night he slept like a baby, dream-free! In hindsight, his conversation with Falcon three days ago came to mind. Could it be Miliya and his destinies were intertwined? The answer hadn't come forth, but there was nothing he could do but wait until it did. He opened up a folder, pulled out the contents, and slammed his fist on the sheets of paper. Yet again, he must be patient and wait for the answer.

But he was not a patient man.

"More pancakes, Miliya?" Falcon asked. One pancake remained on Miliya's plate from the hot stack of pancakes Mama Louise had served minutes ago.

"Mercy, Falcon, I'm stuffed." She patted her flat stomach. The doctor took a sip of coffee and gazed at his sister. For years, he had believed God would unite him with his family. Even though his parents and grandparents were with the Lord, his sister was here with him. He had rejoiced when she told him God was the Lord of her life.

Falcon closed his eyes. So many times, he wanted to quit believing, quit trusting, but God had a plan to give him a future and hope! He was unaware of the tears settling in his eyes.

His heart expanded with love and compassion for his sister. Last night, after dinner, Falcon escorted Miliya to his home, Falcon Crest, ten minutes from the main house. There siblings shared with her their individual life stories and memories. Miliya wept when she heard his emotional narration of their father's death and how the Kensingtons' love saved him.

Now his sister would experience the brother's love and faithfulness. Falcon had held Miliya in his arms as she told him about the love and security she received from their grandparents. And how their mother died in childbirth, not knowing her father and the pain of losing her mother. They both held each other until the tears had subsided.

"Falcon," Miliya said, but she swallowed her intended words.

When his eyes opened, quelling any conversation, Miliya moved over to Falcon with outstretched arms. He stood as she walked into his warm embrace and hugged his waist, her head resting on his chest. That is how Mama Louise found the sister and brother when she walked into the room. She fought back tears that threatened to run down her cheeks. A few seconds passed before the housekeeper alerted the siblings of her presence.

"Ahem."

The pair turned around. They hadn't heard her enter. Smiling, Falcon raised his sister's chin with his hand to meet her blue gaze.

"Are you all right?"

"Fine."

He nodded and turned to Mama Louise. Miliya sat down at the table.

"Has Nakai had breakfast?"

"No, Falcon. Early this morning he rode out to the north pasture with Royce to check on a broken fence."

"Kayja is in the parlor."

"Thank you, Mama Louise. Tell her we're coming." The older woman pulled out a handkerchief from her skirt and dabbed her eyes as she left the room.

"Who is Kayja?" his sister asked.

"My Uncle John's daughter. She is our cousin but acts like our mother. Come and meet her."

He walked towards the door, and a nervous Miliya followed behind him.

More family? Will she accept me? Why not? She must ignore this fear of rejection! A second later, she received her answer.

"Welcome, cousin!" a female voice exclaimed. A young woman rose from the sofa as soon as the siblings stepped through the door. Miliya found herself in a tight embrace, and then just as fast, she was released. Beaming, the exuberant young woman gave Falcon a peck on his cheek.

"Now, look what you have done; she's purple!" Falcon reprimanded the woman and shook his head at her enthusiastic greeting. Concern present in her hazel eyes, Kayja observed the young woman. ....

"Hello. My name is Miliya. My brother thinks he's a comedian."

Her gaze shifted to Falcon, who displayed an innocent look as he flashed a small smile.

His cousin rolled her eyes, slapped him on his shoulder, and then turned back to Miliya with warm, hazel eyes.

"My name is Kayja, their darling cousin. At least, someone in this family had manners." Once again, Kayja rolled her eyes at Falcon. He shrugged his wide shoulders.

"If you hadn't mugged her as soon as she walked in, I would have introduced her," Falcon grinned.

"Humph! He thinks he's funny! Royce is the jokester of the brothers. Each one has different mannerisms. Let's sit down and get acquainted." She moved over to one end of the sofa and Miliya the opposite. Kayja eyed Falcon with lifted brows.

"You sir, go wash some of your instruments or something."

"Madame, I am affronted!" Falcon said. "I will take my leave!" With long strides, he headed out the front door.

"He's adorable." Kayja winked at Miliya. "I feel as though I know you already. You have been the subject of this house for the past week. Falcon was so excited when he learned of your existence."

Miliya blushed.

"I didn't mean to embarrass you," Kayja said in response to the rosy glow spreading over the young woman's face. "He told us about you with tears in his eyes. I've never seen him happier."

"I am grateful the Kensington family has accepted me," Miliya said. "With the grace of God, we'll have until eternity to know and love each other."

"Now that you are part of this family, you need to know that the Kensingtons love, protect, and take care of their own."

Miliya thought of how the four brothers had helped Falcon to apprehend the abductors who had held her captive.

"I love them like brothers," Kayja said.

"Who do you love, Kayja?" A husky voice asked.

An attractive, nut-brown man in his late thirties looked at both women with a warm smile on his face.

Without answering, Kayja stood and walked into the man's open arms. "I love you, silly." She leaned back. Her gaze bored into him with adoration. "I want to introduce you to Falcon's sister." She turned to the young woman. "Miliya, my husband, Lucas Adams."

Kayja stepped out of her husband's arms to allow him to extend a hand in greeting.

"Welcome to the family, Miliya." His wide grin revealed even, white teeth. She stood and received his proffered hand.

"Thank you, Lucas." *Are all the men giants in this town?*

A slight movement from the doorway snagged Kayja's eye. Her smile radiated. Nakai had entered the room and stood against the wall with arms crossed and a small curl on his lips.

"Nakai?" his cousin walked over to him, and his dark eyes softened.

"Kayja." He leaned and kissed the top of her head; the slight curl curved into a welcome smile.

"Good morning, Nakai."

His brows furrowed, Nakai turned at her cheerful voice. Miliya couldn't help but smile at the wariness in his dark eyes. *Did he think she was angry with him from yesterday?* Last night, she had visited her brother's home and had returned to the guest house a little past midnight. *Did Nakai look for her?* Reacting to her smile, he strolled over and drew her into his arms.

"Good morning!" His voice was deep. "Forgive me, Miliya for my callousness yesterday." He whispered low for her ears only. "I would have apologized last night, but you were at Falcon Crest.

My action was not becoming of a big brother. I'll do my best not to repeat such behavior in the future."

"You're forgiven, Nakai."

All-consuming ebony eyes lingered on her face before he released his hold.

"Mr. Nakai Kensington," Kayja called, "Come back to earth. Are you all right?"

His cousin misses nothing, Miliya thought. What does that perplexing frown etched on his face mean?

Calling her by her childhood nickname, Nakai answered, "Just fine, Kay."

"Well then, let's get down to business." His cousin sat on the sofa and joined by her husband and Miliya. Nakai, a formidable figure clad in black pants and a white shirt, stood and leaned against the wall.

"Is this a family meeting?" Falcon asked as he strode into the room. "Hey, big brother, everything straight at the north pastures?" He sat next to his sister.

Nakai nodded. "The fence was down, Royce and the guys fixed it."

"Falcon, I declare you have a charming sister. What happened to you?" Lucas winked at Miliya.

"Many have told me I am irresistible." He waggled his thick brows.

"Must be your delusional female patients," Lucas joked.

"I see his generous heart." Miliya placed her hand on Falcon's chest.

Kayja responded. "Pay them no mind, Miliya. They're incorrigible at times."

"Only a beloved sister can love that face." Lucas said. His wife poked her husband in his side.

"You're right on time," Kayja announced.

"For what?"

The brothers eyed their cousin.

"I've spoken to Royce, Dakota, and Raven about this matter already." She was twitching in her seat with eager excitement.

Falcon and Nakai exchanged glances and shook their heads. The last time she included the brothers in one of her programs was to tell them (her way of asking) to be models at a charity fashion show given by the church's Missionary Committee. That Sunday the committee announced two thousand dollars was collected because of the infamous Kensington brothers participation.

"A party! We will host a get-together to introduce Miliya to our friends and family on Saturday. That's tomorrow. We've much work to do!"

Falcon groaned, Nakai lifted both eyebrows, Lucas grinned, and Miliya grimaced.

Miliya was nervous! Tonight was the get-together Kayja and Louise had arranged in her honor to meet the friends of the family. Falcon took her to Miriam's Dress Shop to make a few purchases for the event. According to Kayja, they stocked the latest fashions from New York and Paris. Shopping was not her forte, but she wanted to make a good impression, so she purchased a new outfit and undergarments for the occasion.

After making her selections, Falcon shocked her when he told her he had opened an account for her. He explained he could afford any expenditures she made. Now, he had a chance to love, protect, and provide for his sister.

She had embraced him and thanked God for her brother. In the back of her mind, she thought of ways to repay his kindness.

Looking into the full-length mirror, Miliya was captivated by the woman in the blue silk dress. She added pearl earrings and slipped her feet into the blue silk slippers to complete the outfit. A soft rap on the door resonated.

Patting the pinned-up curls atop her head, Miliya called out. "Come in." Miliya called out. She heard the front door of the guest house open and shut. She was expecting her brother Falcon, who was to escort her to the affair.

Her brother entered the room and stood transfixed as he gazed upon his sister. Shaking his head, he advanced towards her.

"Is there something wrong with my dress?" All the while, she scanned her reflection in the mirror.

"Nothing is wrong with your attire, sister," he whispered. "Your loveliness is radiant. I brought you a gift."

Falcon withdrew a black satin box from his jacket pocket and opened it. An exquisite short pearl necklace lay elegantly atop the cream satin velvet. Excited, Miliya gasped. Her brother fastened it around her neck, then stepped back, and his approval. The lustrous pearls complemented the low vee neckline.

Brother and sister embraced each other before Miliya said, "Thank you, Falcon."

Falcon smiled. "You are a blessing to me, and I love you." He kissed her on her forehead.

"I love you too."

Smiling, Falcon released his hold on his sister. "Are you ready to meet Pinedale's finest?" The young woman nodded.

"You present a handsome picture brother."

Miliya complimented. He wore a tailored gray vested suit, white shawl-collared shirt, and black tie.

"Thank you, Madame." She slipped her arm into his.

"I know you approve, and that is my main concern, but will they?" she asked, trying not to sound or look fearful.

"Be yourself, Miliya. Your warmth and gentle spirit are attributes acceptable to all. Remember, I love you, and so do the Kensingtons." The siblings exited the room, confident all would be well this night.

CHAPTER 6

"Is that her?"
"She too light-skinned to be his sister."
"They say he's got white blood in him."
"Well, she sure is pretty!"

Nakai shook his head at the whispered, bias remarks spreading through the bevy of people. Why must there be a comparison of skin color if one is a product of two races? He understood the plight of the Indian and the Negro.

The white man possessed an exorbitant degree of hate and greed interconnected with prejudice and a sense of nobility. They seized Indian lands, slaughtered their women and children while forcibly commandeering Negroes in chains from their homeland for the sole purpose to be bound in servitude as if this treatment was the natural order of things. No human being had the right to own or control another human being. God is the Master and Creator of all mankind, and we are his children. But Nakai was intelligent enough to know bigots existed.

"Our brother has introduced Miliya to everyone but the flowers on the tables." Dakota grinned. The brothers watched Falcon introduce Miliya to Kayja's parents, Daniel and Susie Kensington.

"As usual, our little cousin did an outstanding job decorating," Raven said as he admired the ten round tables situated around the room.

A basket of assorted, fresh flowers adorned the center of the table, covered with a white linen tablecloth. Positioned in a corner, four young men filled the air with music ranging from ballads to Ragtime.

The brothers, assisted by Kayja, held the affair at the Kensington Hall, an added addition to the main house, to accommodate a capacity of one hundred people. They usually used the vast room for family and business affairs.

"I'm surprised she doesn't have us taking part in one of her crazy fundraising ideas," Royce smirked.

"Whenever she includes us, we get the short end of the stick." Dakota squared his ankle over one knee. "For instance, remember last month when she told us, her way of asking, to buy raffle tickets for new church pews?"

With a hint of a smile on his lips, Royce reminisced about last month's fiasco. "Sure do. We told her we would give a large donation, but no raffle tickets! She fell to her knees, begging, even dropped a few tears. But when we stood our ground, she conceded and told the truth."

Raven bobbed his head. "The winners would share a picnic lunch with one of Pinesdale's bachelors, including us! Our darling cousin slipped our names in the box."

Laughing, Royce shook his head. "Once the tickets were removed, Raven supervised all entries to make sure there were no tickets with the Kensington name on it. Our little Kay was livid!"

Dakota grinned. "The savage look on our Cheyenne brother's face was the reason Mayor Johnson's hand trembled every time he withdrew a ticket. he rumor around town was his arthritis flared up!" Raven joined his brothers' in laughter.

Nakai sent them a sullen look. They knew their older brother didn't take to teasing. His sense of humor left with Zelia two years ago.

"No one tells me who to spend my time with!" Nakai scowled. He ignored his brothers and scanned the crowd for Falcon and Miliya.

Pure joy covered Falcon's face as he introduced his sister to Pastor Dave and his wife Sara. Nakai felt a pang of guilt. Through the past year, his body attended church, but his mind was absent when the sermon dealt with love and marriage.

Nakai blamed Zelia Jensen. He knew he must forgive her faithlessness and go on with his life. To do otherwise was to deny the responsibility the Divine connection God had for him in the future. The word stunning came to mind as he watched Miliya in the blue silk creation accompany Falcon to where Kayja and Lucas stood.

In this instance, the band began playing a lively song.

"Seems like our guest of honor has every bachelor in attendance formed in a line for a dance," Raven observed.

"I told you there would be an upheaval amongst the single men vying for Miliya's attention." Amazement laced Royce's voice.

Nakai's jaw clenched. Men lined up like they were dying from thirst, and Miliya was water!

"I'm headed over to the comely Laurel Johnson for a dance." Dakota nodded to his brothers and strolled off, unaware of the swooning females as he passed by.

"Is Sebastian King here?" Raven looked around the room.

"No, he left last week for Denver to visit his brother Tyler. He said he would be home tonight." Nakai rubbed his chin.

Raven nodded. "I'm going over to the refreshment table. You want some iced tea?"

"No. I'm in the mood to dance," Nakai said. His dark eyes narrowed. Hoping to get close enough to devour Miliya with their senseless talk, men surrounded her like vultures hovering over their prey. Without another word, he stalked towards the guest of honor and her devoted worshippers.

Royce and Raven exchanged bemused looks. The brothers had attended many functions in the past year, and Nakai never danced, not even with their female relatives. Was he heading for Miliya?

Where is Falcon? Miliya glanced around the crowded room, searching for a reprieve from the onslaught of Pinesdale's eager bachelors. If one more person stepped on her toes, she'd say, "Excuse me," and run off the floor.

"Miss, my name is Clyde Miller. May I have this dance?"

Distracted from her thoughts, Miliya turned around. Behind her stood an average height medium-frame young man with unremarkable sable features. Her feet shouted, no, but the word lodged in her throat. Bewildered, Miliya watched wide-eyed as the owner of the Kensington Estate stalked towards them. The crowd of male admirers dispersed as the intimidating figure Nakai Kensington approached. No doubt, the man was irritated. At her? But why?

With a forced smile, the man at Miliya's side said, "Evening, Sir," as Nakai approached.

Before turning to her, the formidable man answered the nervous young man.

"Clyde."

Miliya gazed at him in time to witness a disarming smile light up his bronze face. Hmm, what does he want?

"Dance with me," Nakai said to Miliya.

Clyde's arm disrupted her response. He tapped Nakai on his shoulder. Turning around, Nakai glared at the young man.

Clyde swallowed hard. "It's my turn." Nakai cocked his head to the side. Coal-black, fierce eyes slammed into Clyde's. He impressed Miliya with a determination to hold his position under the tenacious scrutiny of the older man.

"Really?" Nakai advanced towards Clyde.

"Nakai," Miliya placed her hand on his arm, "Mr. Miller has waited in line for a dance. It will be my pleasure to dance with you after him."

Glowering, Nakai glanced down at her hand on his arm; his eyes softened.

"As you wish." He bowed. Jet eyes hardened when he faced Clyde. "Take your turn. " He spoke the words in a low, menacing voice and then stepped aside. The young man released a whoosh of air, straightened his stance, and then approached Miliya. Nakai watched Clyde pull Miliya into his arms. Nakai's fist clenched, but he doesn't move until his intense gaze captured and locked her eyes with his. She missed a step and frowned. The corner of Nakai's mouth lifted as they melted into the crowd of dancers.

Royce stood shocked at the scene that had unfurled across the room. His older brother almost clobbered Clyde Miller. Why? The poor guy wanted to dance with Miliya, but so did Nakai! When Miliya spoke to him, touched his arm, and gave him that enchanting smile, he retreated. No one, male or female, had the power to affect his actions as Miliya just did. Could it be after two years of meaningless relationships, one woman has piqued his interest enough to cause him to fight for love? Big brother better take heed, or the newest member of the Kensington family would mend that shattered heart.

Could that be a good thing?

CHAPTER 7

Clyde Miller was a thirty-three-year-old single man, employed as a clerk at the Pinesdale Community Bank and a faithful member of Mount Bethel Church. As he continued to ply Miliya with stories of bank clerks and onerous duties, boredom coaxed her to peer around the opulent room. Polished hardwood floors, electric lights, and wall-to-wall burgundy drapes boasted extravagance. Baskets of fragrant flowers flourished as centerpieces on tables draped in white linen and added ambiance to the room. Raised on a farm and living in a modest two-story house, Miliya couldn't fathom such luxury. But it was the way of life for the Kensington's. She spotted Royce and Dakota surrounded by several young ladies, each vying for their attention. The brothers were not only fine-looking men but also well respected in the community. Her azure gaze continued searching the crowd. She spotted Falcon and Nakai in deep conversation standing against the wall. Her brows furrowed. Judging from the laxness of his body Nakai appeared to have gained control of his anger. Thank God. She conceded earlier when he approached her his arrogant manner had unnerved her. The man could be sweet, but also intimidating. Did anyone else notice these fetching qualities?

She was unaccustomed to such character imperfections, but everyone had a flaw or two, so she just had to skirt around the big man, in hopes he remembered she was his sister and treated her as such.

"Ugh!" Clyde stepped on her toe.

"Miliya, I'm sorry. I've two left feet."

"More like three!" She ignored the pinched look on his face. Her toes throbbed.

When Clyde began laughing, Miliya chimed in.

Falcon had sauntered over to Nakai, standing against the wall, his striking face absorbed in thought.

"What's going on, brother?"

"What do you mean?" Nakai lifted a brow. His intense glare lingered on Miliya as she laughed at something Clyde said. Falcon did not miss the tic in his brother's eye. Did Nakai and Clyde have a dispute over banking matters? What could have transpired between them to call for this odd behavior from his usually passive brother?

"Your self-control over your anger. For a split second, I thought Mr. Miller would need my services." Falcon exhaled.

"Humph!" Nakai snorted. "Still may."

"What did he do to upset your usual sunny manner?" Falcon suppressed a smile and crossed his arms over his chest.

Nakai met his baffled gaze. "That man is dancing with my blue-eyed, elusive woman."

Baffled, Falcon uncrossed his arms and regarded his brother. What had Nakai just said?

Nakai inclined his head. "Your sister is the angelic being from my dreams."

The doctor shook his head in disbelief. What does this mean, Lord? Is your plan at work in Nakai's life? Can Miliya unlock the cast-iron box that encloses his heart? Falcon had so many unanswered questions. Please enlighten me, Lord, with the answers. I love them both and trust in your timing to reveal your plan for their lives.

He glanced over at his sister and saw her gaze locked on Nakai. This was the second time he noticed the byplay between the two. The first time was last night in the parlor and now. Could there be an attraction?

"I don't mean any disrespect toward you or Miliya, but she invaded my dreams every night, and now she's here. Alive and in person, dancing with a person who wants to yap, yap, and drool all over her." His deep voice escalated.

"Brother calm down. Jealousy doesn't look good on you. You're acting like a caged up bear." Nakai was unaware he was clenching and unclenching his fists. Falcon patted Nakai on his broad back. "Remember our conversation a few days ago when you told me about your mysterious vision?" He didn't wait for a reply but continued, "Do you recall my advice about your situation?"

Nakai inhaled a deep breath. "You said trust in God to work things out."

Falcon nodded. "There is a reason Miliya entered our lives other than the death of our grandmother. God knows why, and when He is ready to reveal the reason, He will." He cleared his throat. "Here comes your elusive woman."

Miliya made her way towards the men. She acknowledged her brother then addressed Nakai. "Dance with me?"

How could he resist her sweet smile and guileless blue eyes? "My pleasure." Nakai said.

He received her extended hand and led her to the floor among the other dancers.

"What's going on?" Royce wanted to know. He and his brothers had observed the interaction between Miliya and Nakai. They walked over to find out what had happened.

"Divine intervention," Falcon responded.

Later that night…

Miliya sat up in the bed. She couldn't sleep. Tonight, she enjoyed a delightful time at the get-together; however, her feet had their own opinion. She had danced with close to twenty men tonight, and at least ten stepped on her toes. Clyde Miller was the worst. If he would have kept his eyes on what he was doing instead of glancing around to see where Nakai was, he may have saved her toes some unnecessary pain. However, she understood his fear of the man. Nakai could be authoritative, but her feet were tired of being trampled on, so without a thought, she ended the torture. As they moved to a ballad, she had whispered near Clyde's ear, "Hello, Nakai."

The man froze immobile on her foot and whipped his head around to look over his shoulder. She realized it wasn't a ladylike action, but her feet begged her to end the constant pain. With a murmured "Excuse me," Clyde held his crotch and danced a frantic jig to the bathroom, fully aware of the puddle his anxiety left behind. The young man didn't return and soon left the party.

Embarrassed for him, she had sauntered over to where Nakai and Falcon stood to claim her dance. Did this man know his demeanor was unsettling? When he had touched her hand, she

felt an uneasiness to the degree she wanted to snatch it back. Once he started a conversation and apologized again, the unease toned down to a warm sensation throughout her body until the dance ended. Strange.

Midnight at the Estate

Dreams do come true. At least, tonight his did, Nakai told himself, as he sat on the edge of his four-poster bed. He made a mental note to add "fair and considerate" to his list of her assets. In his dreams, he had enjoyed her presence with uninhibited behavior, and God help him, he desired the same in his waking hours. Lord, it was hard being her brother! Tonight, when Miliya asked him to dance, his heartbeat had quickened when she smiled up at him. When he held her at a proper distance, a sense of peace engulfed his entire being. For a few seconds, they had swayed to the ballad until he broke the silence. Her body had tensed.

"Thank you for the dance, Miliya." He noticed her almond-hued skin turned red from blushing. Those slanted blue eyes ogled his chest. He remembered thinking she appeared fearful. Of him? Was she still upset over the occurrence that happened at breakfast when he acted like a complete fool? Maybe she didn't think his first apology was sincere.

"Miliya, I am sorry and embarrassed for my actions towards you the other morning. Do you believe I was genuine?"

She had raised her eyes to his for a second before speaking. "I have accepted your apology and have forgiven you. It is done." A charming smile had developed on her lips, and he felt her body relax.

He would let God handle their relationship. For now, he'd be her oldest brother. For now.

CHAPTER 8

Pastor Owens finished his sermon on the Holy Spirit in a record time of forty-five minutes instead of the usual hour. After services, the pastor and his wife would visit their daughter and her family in Hardwick. The trip would take a day's ride, and they wanted to be there by nightfall. Mrs. Ross, the church clerk, finished reading the announcements and sat down. Taking his cue, Pastor Owens stepped down from the pulpit.

"Last night, Mrs. Owen and I attended a gathering at the Kensington Estate to meet our esteemed Doctor Falcon's estranged sister, Miliya. Please join me in welcoming this young lady to our church and community. Oh, by the way, single men, she's not married! Sister Miliya, please stand."

Sounds of male applause resonated two towns away. Oh goodness! If she could, Miliya would have melted down into her shoes and run out of there. Applause erupted as she stood blushing. She quickly sat back down and released a long sigh of relief.

After services, Kayja introduced her brothers Jace and Daniel. Both men were a head shorter than their cousins. They each had brown eyes with flecks of green, thick, black hair that hugged their heads in cropped waves, and attractive features. A group of young ladies sashayed past, gave tiny waves, and avoided any eye contact. Miliya smiled. Yes, they have the Kensington charm.

Kayja excused herself and hailed Pastor Owen, leaving Miliya standing alone. She scanned the crowded church grounds for Falcon until she located him and the other brothers under a tree where they were laughing and talking with Luke and another man. Two young women strolled by and spoke to Royce. When he responded with a dimpled smile, they fanned themselves senseless with their lace handkerchiefs. Amused, Miliya shook her head.

In the time, as a member of the Kensington family, she clearly understood why women hankered after the brothers, or the K5, a name she had overheard several of the women call them. The simple truth was the Kensington brothers were the epitome of masculinity, power, and exceptional good looks. The first thing one noticed was they all stood over six feet, and their facial features-chiseled noses, high cheekbones, and full-shaped lips-hinted at a mixed ancestry. They all possessed well-defined, muscular bodies. Royce, the youngest at 32, with hazel eyes, tanned skin, curly black hair an inch or two above his shoulder was the family jokester and her champion.

Then Dakota, 34, his skin tone a smidgen darker than Royce's, had light brown eyes and thick, black wavy hair tied back in a queue. He was sensible and reserved. Her darling brother, Falcon, 35, and the spiritual one of the brothers had misty gray eyes that changed to the color of twilight shadows. His skin was a deep tan, and his black, wavy hair hung to his shoulders. Raven, 36, the sheriff was the only one to have olive-green eyes. His skin hue was between an almond and tan and accented by straight, dark brown hair that touched the collar of his shirt.

Last, Nakai, 37, stoic and unpredictable, was a full-blooded Cheyenne with bronze skin and the tallest at six-six. His piercing eyes that deepened according to the events of his day reminded her of rich coffee. Satin, black hair fell just below his broad shoulders.

They were men of faith, a family well respected in the community and among their peers. She was thankful they included her in their lives. Glancing around the churchyard, she noticed most of the congregation had departed to their homes to partake in their Sunday dinners.

"Scuse me, Miss." A swarthy-skinned man dressed in a well-worn brown suit, clenching a weather-beaten hat in his hand staggered towards Miliya. They had introduced her to many people, but she did not recognize him.

"Yes." Her wide smile faltered. Was that liquor she smelled? She placed her senses on alert.

"Preacher man says you are available for marriage." His speech slurred.

What?

"He said I was single. I'm not looking to marry you or anyone else." There! She couldn't have said it any plainer! The man stepped closer, and the stench of alcohol nearly overwhelmed her.

"Look woman, the Preacher wouldn't lie. He said you're available, and I needs me a woman." He grabbed her wrist and jerked her forward.

Lord, not on the church grounds! "Mister, please, don't make me hurt you!"

"C'mon, woman. We, marrying up right now!" His grip tightened on her arm as he reached for the other arm. She lifted her right leg

61

and forced a knee into his groin. He fell to the ground howling like a wounded animal as he held his genitals. Strong arms enveloped her.

"Stop struggling, sis. It's me."

"I didn't want to hurt him, Royce, but he could have hurt me." Her raspy voice quivered. "I'm sorry. I didn't mean to embarrass your family." Tears streamed down her face. Most of the congregation had left, and the brothers reassured the few members that mulled about of her well-being.

This wasn't the first time a man wanted to claim her. She blamed it on her looks. That's why she liked to be in the background, away from the center of attention. But Psalm 139: 14 resounded in her mind. "I am fearfully and wonderfully made." She was how God created her to be.

"Miliya!" Falcon pulled her out of Royce's arms and into his. "Shh, stop crying. I'm here."

Through her tears, she saw Raven, Dakota, and Royce had circled them.

"We're sorry we didn't get to you sooner, but it happened so fast. One minute, you're standing by yourself, and the next Ed Masters had accosted you." Raven glared at the man stumbling toward the horses and buggies. Dakota looked at his younger brother. "We haven't seen Royce move that fast since Dad caught him in the barn kissing Mary Jane Smith."

"The man was drunk. He lost his wife last year to heart problems, and he's been drinking ever since," Falcon explained. He looked down at his sister. "Are you feeling better?"

"Yes. I'm fine." He released his arms.

"Where is Nakai?" Miliya asked. The four men looked at each other.

"Our friend Bash took him home," Falcon said. His grays changed to silver. What wasn't he telling her?

"Why?" The men looked like four young boys with a secret.

"What aren't you telling me?"

Her champion volunteered the explanation. "Bash took Nakai home, or else he would have killed Ed."

The only thing she said was, "Oh."

CHAPTER 9

Sebastian King, "Bash," his childhood nickname, sat on the love seat in the upstairs office of his close friend who stood rigid and staring out the window.

"What got into you today, Nakai? If I didn't force you on your horse and hightail it out of there, you would have killed that man! What made you go for your knife?" Bash had referred to the sheathed Bowie strapped to Nakai's leg.

"Because I didn't have a gun!" Nakai growled.

"A gun?" Bash shook his head. "My friendship with you and your brothers extend over twenty years. Growing up we were inseparable, that's why people called us Bash and the "K5", remember?" Sebastian stared at the stiff, wide shoulders of his friend as he gazed out the window.

"K5" are men of integrity, strength, and trustworthiness. Nakai, everyone knows you are a force to be reckoned with if anyone touches a hair on your loved ones' heads, but the murderous look in your eyes scared me today. Not like you, my friend." Bash walked over to the window and stared out. Flanked by three of his brothers on horseback, Falcon had just pulled the carriage up in front of the Estate. Handing the reins to a ranch hand, he ambled to the other side where Miliya sat and assisted her from the carriage.

Bash sucked in his breath. She was beautiful! Late last night he had returned from Denver from visiting his brother Tyler and wasn't able to attend the gathering Saturday, so today was the first time seeing "K5's" newest family member. From his view, the sun's rays had filtered slivers of gold throughout her honey-brown hair flowing past her shoulders. The emerald green dress she wore complimented her light complexion. He was hoping to have met her at church if only to see the amazing blue eyes the men were in an uproar about. It was almost as though she heard his thoughts, for her gaze drifted up towards the window. A fleeting moment. Time froze before she grinned and waved.

A frown crossed Bash's face. He glanced sideways at Nakai, his ebon gaze fixed on the young woman, and lifted his chin. The young woman acknowledged and then allowed Falcon to escort her to the guesthouse. Startled by what he saw, Bash faced his friend with raised brows. "Now I see why you acted the way you did," he said as he watched Falcon and Miliya enter the guesthouse. "But you can't allow your emotions to cloud your judgment."

Nakai studied his friend with eyes that flashed black lightning. Slowly, deliberately, he cocked his head then he spoke a calm, deadly tone. "What do you mean 'I see why?' What do you think you saw?"

A sense of foreboding rushed over Bash; he must tread with care. Nakai was holding something deep within that resisted any entrance into that part of him. For now, he would leave the matter alone. Bash held both his hands up in surrender.

"In due time. Until then when can I meet Miliya?" A smile spread over his smooth-shaven features. Nakai winked at him.

"When I say so, and not a second sooner." And for the first time in a long time, the eldest Kensington brother laughed.

Miliya could not relax. She gazed out the bedroom window and admired the broad moon: round, brilliant and majestic against the midnight sky, an effect of the eternal handiwork of God. The thin cotton nightgown she wore held no relief from the humid July night. She ambled out onto the porch and stumbled upon the cushioned seat. Her dexterous fingers weaved waist-length hair into a honey brown braid and slipped it over her shoulder to rest on her lap. Moans of comfort filled her throat as a hint of a breeze kissed her neck.

Curious, she peered over at the Estate and sighted a light beaming from Nakai's room. Guess she wasn't the only one who couldn't sleep. Was he thinking about the day's occurrences? All evening, she kept thinking about the incident with Ed Masters. A man drunk with haunting memories, searching for love, in the wrong way.

When he had snatched her arm, it triggered her defense mechanism, and she had reacted. Grandpa Peter would have been proud of the immediate and efficient manner she had taken her assailant to the task.

At first, the brothers were unaware of her plight, but once Mr. Master's loudly revealed his intentions Royce had reached her first within seconds, followed by the other three men. They enveloped her in a cocoon of love. As for Nakai, did he really want to kill the man because of her?

Later, Royce said if Bash hadn't stopped his brother from accosting Mr. Masters, Nakai would have done real damage to him, maybe fatal damage. She understood his responsibility to protect his family, but for her?

Then she realized; Nakai thought of her as a member of the family! All doubts and insecurities of fitting in with this family melted like butter in a hot skillet. Nakai had extended a family friend Sebastian King, a dinner invitation which he had eagerly accepted. When he entered the dining room, the first thing she noticed was he exuded confidence, charisma, and magnetism, a man who knows what he wants and how to get it. He was rangy, about six-three, smooth pecan-colored skin, light brown eyes, and sported a head ladened with black tight curls. Tonight, at dinner, she had felt uneasy. Something odd happened after she left the dining room with Bash. She sat cross legged on the bench recreating the evening's occurrences.

After dinner, she enjoyed the bantering between the brothers and Bash. Nakai threw in a joke here and there. Feeling a bit intrusive, she decided to step out on the porch to watch the sunset. When there was a lull in the conversation, she rose from her seat, and the six men did likewise.

"Retiring so soon, Miliya?" Bash asked.

She responded, "Not yet. I'm going to watch the stars ignite the evening sky from the porch. It's a beautiful sight."

"Yes, beautiful." His eyes never left her face. "May I join you?"

A low rumble emanated from his side. All eyes turned to Nakai, all except Bash's.

"May I, Miliya?" Soft brown eyes widened in hope. Blazing fury darkened Nakai's face. The brothers looked concerned, but Falcon had closed his eyes. Was he praying?

The tense silence in the room had been stifling. She questioned why the bewilderment on the brothers' faces, and why Nakai resembled a demon from the pit of hell?

No matter what the reason, Sebastian King appeared to be a gentleman, and she admired his demeanor. Besides, knowing the boys, they had already informed him what she would do to his manhood if she felt threatened.

After Miliya told Bash he could join her, he had placed her arm in his, and they proceeded to the porch. Sounds of chairs overturning, rumbling noises, and raised voices resonated from behind them as Bash ushered her onto the porch and closed the door. Once seated on the rocker, she had asked, "What was that noise?"

"Sounds like a wild dog got loose in the house. Nothing to worry about," he had assured her as he glanced warily at the door.

Miliya sat on the bench and thought about Bash's response to her question. A wild dog? Growling noises? Loose in the house? As far as she knew, the brothers didn't own a dog. Somehow, she sensed he was communicating a message through his words. Okay, let's take this step by step. She recalled the light-hearted bantering among the men, and then she went on the porch. Bash asked to join her. Silence, but a low snarling sound emanated from his side. Nakai sat next to Bash. She bolted upright in her seat. Nakai was the wild dog?

When they had returned inside, nothing seemed amiss, except for Nakai. Falcon said he had returned to his office. She concluded the oldest brother was too protective of her. Even her other champions, Royce and Falcon, her biological brother, weren't that possessive, and Nakai's overprotective ways had to stop. Bash was a gentleman with a sense of humor and, in time, a good friend.

One day, a special man would enter her life. Did she have to worry an overzealous brother will shoot him?

Miliya released a long sigh. Her prayer tonight would include the issue. She would wait for God's instruction. Miliya gazed up at the office window, now dark as the night.

Yawning, she rose from the bench and entered the guesthouse, slamming the door behind her.

The wide-shouldered man sat atop the white stallion in the shadows. His sable eyes focused on the young woman entering the house. The minutes ticked by before the man and the horse galloped away, vanishing into the night.

CHAPTER 10

Nakai covered his head with the sheet, trying to drown out the continuous pounding on his bedroom door. He peeked over at the grandfather clock standing at attention against the wall. Who dared to bang on his door at 8:30 in the morning? Throwing back the sheet, he stumbled from the bed and clutched his bathrobe. In his haste, he stubbed his toe against the bedside stand. Now he was livid!

Nakai wrenched the door open. The four Kensington brothers stood grinning at him.

"What?" He grappled for control over his tongue unless he said something he'd regret afterward. "You four had better have a good reason for interrupting my sleep," Nakai grumbled as he tightened the sash on his robe.

"Thanks for welcoming us in, big brother." Royce walked past a fuming Nakai into the room. Raven, Dakota, and Falcon followed him. Nakai slammed the door with such force the oil painting of his white stallion, Lightning, plummeted to the floor.

Royce shook his head. "Now, look at what you've done." A playful grin blossomed on his lips. Nakai raked through his unruly hair with strong brown fingers. Sighing, he sat down on the four-poster bed. "What do you want from me?" He slowly enunciated each word.

"Are. You. Craaazy?" Royce smirked.

Nakai rolled his eyes at them before directing his glowering eyes at his younger brother. "Crazy? You want crazy?" Nakai flew from the bed, but Falcon quickly gripped his brother's shoulder and nudged him backward on the bed.

"Royce! Enough!" Gray eyes met twinkling hazel. Sobering, the young man nodded. Falcon pulled up an armchair across from Nakai. With raised eyebrows he turned to his brothers.

"We'll stand," Dakota glanced around at Raven and Royce.

"Suit yourselves," Falcon said. He turned to Nakai, leaned forward in the chair, and announced. "This is a family meeting. Your unusual actions of late concern us, and we hoped together we can resolve the issue." The silence was deafening.

Nakai ran his hand over his face. He studied each brother with his dark gaze.

Sensible Falcon, the one with a calm demeanor, would be the mediator. Raven was fair and family orientated, Dakota was loyal to a fault, and, Royce, the youngest, spoke his mind, loved life, was easygoing, and a thorn in Nakai's side.

This was an intervention

"Unusual?" Royce retorted. "Chairs flying, with us in them, a heavy oak dining room table overturned is unusual, but when you roared like a grizzly bear, that brother is crazy!" He ignored the frowns on his brothers' faces. With lifted brows, Nakai focused his intense

eyes on Royce. His slow, determined steps crossed the room to where his youngest brother was leaning against the wall. All the while, he was aware the alert eyes of the others followed his every step. He smiled as Royce, his eyes enlarged, straightened his body to his full six-foot-two height.

"Little brother," Nakai began, "I admit to the lunacy yesterday, and I apologize to each one of you." He expressed genuine regret.

Royce released a long sigh of relief, glad the strained moment was over.

"What's troubling you, Nakai?" Raven asked the robed man standing with arms crossed.

How can he tell them Miliya means more to him than an adopted sister? That, in no way he can be the brother she expected? There were no words in any language that could point out the passionate emotions he felt for Miliya. This thought frightened him.

"Whatever it is we are family. We'll work it out together," Raven said from behind him.

"Yes, no matter what it is," Dakota asserted.

"I think I know what his problem is." The four brothers shifted their eyes to meet the solemn face of their younger brother.

"What's that?" Nakai asked in a flat voice. Royce cleared his throat.

"At the get-together, you acted like you would smash Clyde's face when he approached Miliya to dance. If she hadn't touched your arm to calm you, the clerk would have been a dark spot on the wall. Then on the church grounds, Bash hogtied you to your horse, or else Ed Masters would be with his wife in heaven today! Tell me, does a man dancing with a female family member be a justifiable reason to murder a man?"

A blanket of silence covered the room. No one blinked. Looks of astonishment appeared on the men's faces. The sober appearance of his brother did not display the rage churning within Nakai. Glaring at Royce, he sat down on the bed. His brother was too astute for his well-being.

"Are you insinuating Nakai has deeper feelings for Miliya other than a brother's love?" Raven frowned, his voice threaded with unbelief.

Everyone turned their attention to Royce. "Do chickens lay eggs?"

he asked.

"Nakai is her protector, the same way we are." Raven peered at the bowed Nakai's bowed head. His next words would be the catalyst to discerning the truth.

"Mister King seems smitten with our Miliya. They would make the perfect couple." Raven observed the bowed head jerk up with eyes black and raging.

Falcon noticed the throbbing vein on Nakai's neck. He may have to step in and tell his brothers the truth before the situation escalated.

"Dakota," Raven called with a conspiratorial wink, "did you see how Bash was caressing Miliya's arm as they left the room?"

Dakota nodded, hoping this charade wouldn't cause any trauma.

"Yes. The man looked dazed. Miliya appeared comfortable in his presence."

A chair flew across the room, missing Dakota by inches. In its wake stood an enraged Nakai, his hands clenched by his side.

"Told ya!" Royce declared, jumping around the room.

"I knew it!" Raven yelled.

"I'll be!" Dakota frowned. Disbelief flashed across his face.

Falcon shook his head. Thank God! No bloodshed or broken bones! So far.

"Calm down, everybody," Falcon ordered. "Nakai, sit!" He pointed to the bed, and Nakai reluctantly sat.

"There is a story behind your brother's actions. He should be the one to tell you. I believe you will understand somewhat of what he has been going through." Falcon touched Nakai's shoulder. The secret was out! They know Miliya was the driving force behind his 'crazy' and had been ever since she entered his life.

Just as Raven and Dakota said, they were family. No matter what, they'd be by his side. Nakai faced his brothers and slowly told them his story. When he described his vision and his feelings about her, a clear picture of understanding washed over their features. He ended with a wry smile on his face and a shrug of his massive shoulders. Dakota assessed Nakai before he spoke.

"First, we do not judge you whether your feelings for Miliya are wrong or right. You know your heart, and we know you as a man of integrity and compassion. Two years ago, you were a broken man, and we all hurt with you. Within that time, the anger, hurt, and anguish deep within your soul have lingered. Your laughter is rare, and you smile even less. As far as female companionship, the randy rooster in the henhouse gets more action."

"It's my choice," Nakai grumbled.

"Now, a woman has crossed your path who makes you feel again, maybe love, and, brother, we are glad for you. If you desire to woo her make sure Miliya wants your advances." Dakota nodded and glanced at Raven.

"I agree with Dakota. Our love is with you both. We're here whenever you need us for anything." Raven crossed his arms over his chest and eyed Royce.

"Miliya sees me as her champion. Is that a problem?" Royce

squinted his eyes.

"No problem," Nakai murmured.

"Good. No more flying chairs, toppled tables, and the mad dog howling?"

Nakai sprang from the bed. Raven grabbed Royce by his shoulder and led him out of the room. He released his shoulder and said, "Don't push it, little brother. Wouldn't want a flying chair to hit you, by mistake, of course. Let's go to breakfast."

Royce nodded. He looked back at the bedroom.

"Are you coming?" Raven stood at the head of the stairs.

"Coming." Royce sauntered towards the staircase.

"Has it been two weeks since you arrived in Pinesdale?" Kayja and Miliya sat on the porch of the guest house, drinking lemonade.

"Yes. It has had its moments."

"Do you get along with everybody?"

"Mama Louise is the best. She fusses over me like a mother hen. The brothers are caring, protective, and fun-loving. Nakai is protective." Her eyes lowered.

"Oh? Nakai isn't fun-loving or caring?"

"He's a no-nonsense kind of man and truly protective of family. Very protective."

Miliya murmured the last words under her breath.

"How so?" Kayja asked.

Blushing, Miliya gave her the details of the kitchen incident and the attack at the church.

Kayja's eyes widened. "Did you say murder?"

Miliya nodded.

Kayja's hazel eyes studied the woman sitting on the end of the bench. It was common knowledge her cousin was protective of his family, but to consider murder was extreme!

Kayja recalled the day she had met Falcon's sister and how Nakai had pulled her into his snug embrace and whispered into her ear. His dark eyes had followed her every movement as though in awe of her presence. A slow smile formed on her lips. How could she have missed it? Miliya attracted her cousin as a woman, not a sister. No wonder he's been irrational. He was trying to suppress his feelings, and that was absolute torment!

"Miliya, Nakai is not a murderer. A woman he loved deceived and hurt my cousin, and he wanted to hurt her, but he didn't. So, please, don't judge his character by the incident at the church."

"I am disappointed you would think I judge others using my principles. God is the judge."

"How do you feel about Nakai as a person?" Kayja sat upright on the bench, her eyes questioning.

"Nakai is an impressive man. Underneath the stony exterior is a caring, kind, intelligent person. I pray to the Lord for guidance, safety, and happiness for my brothers, including a special prayer for Nakai. My prayer for him is deliverance from the hurt and anger, which has imprisoned his soul so he can open his unforgiving heart to give unconditional love to that special woman God has chosen for him." Miliya smiled. "Although misunderstood, he has much to give others."

Kayja nodded her head. Little did her friend know she was that woman!

Nakai stared out the train window at the sun-drenched countryside. They had three hours until they reached Pinesdale. On the seat across from him sprawled Dakota, asleep. The noises emerging from his lips did not sound human. Nakai pitied the woman who married him. She would have to be deaf to tolerate those animal sounds. Annoyed, Nakai kicked him with his booted foot. The movement caused Dakota to turn and rest his head against the seat and shelter his face with his hat.

They had delivered four stallions to a buyer in Butte, Montana. Dakota, the estate' veterinarian, accompanied him in case any unseen health problems occurred. Royce would pick them up from the depot. A bath, a meal, and a bed in that order were foremost on Nakai's mind. He closed his eyes and stretched his long legs out on the spot next to his brother. Miliya smiling, appeared, just as she had the previous week. A lovely vision, but pure agony to his mind. After the meeting he had with his brothers, their sure support urged his decision to find out whether she could tolerate more than a cordial relationship. The thought she might reject his advances crossed his mind. Whether their relationships progressed to another level or not, he would always be protective of her.

Intent on daydreaming about the woman who tortured his soul, Nakai leaned backward on the seat and laid his Stetson over his bronze features. Soon, he too was sound asleep.

CHAPTER 11

"Nakai!"

Miliya bolted up from bed, her honey-brown hair tangled about her head like a lustrous halo. For third night in a week, she arose from Nakai's tight embrace as his sculpted lips whispered in her ear, "You are mine!"

The dream began a week ago when Nakai didn't appear for breakfast. Mama Louise told her he and Dakota had left for Butte, Montana, to purchase stallions. Miliya had wavered between disappointment, outrage, and anxiety. Why didn't he mention his intentions to her? He could murder a lonely old man for me, but a simple "I won't be around for a week" was too complicated for him to say?

She plunked back down onto the pillows. What was wrong with her? She was behaving like a lover or a spouse. Besides, she was not his blood relative, so his comings and goings were none of her business.

Miliya glimpsed over at the ornate porcelain clock on the bedstand. The gilded hands displayed 8:00 a.m. Oh, my goodness! She and Bash were going horseback riding this morning at ten afterward return to the estates for lunch.

The same day Nakai left, Bash had invited her to dinner at NICOLE'S, an exclusive French/American restaurant in Pinesdale. The owner Nicolette was a respected friend of Bash and the Kensington brothers. Since she was accepted as the brothers sister, Miliya regarded her as a friend.

She knelt by the bed to say her morning prayers. "Father God, this is the day the Lord has made, and I shall rejoice and be glad in it. I declare this day is in decent and divine order, and I can do all things through Christ that strengthens me. There is no weapon formed against me that shall prosper, my righteousness is of the Lord, and every tongue that should rise against me in judgment, I shall show to be in the wrong. Father, I plead the blood of Jesus to surround my brothers with protection from evil, seen and unseen. Give Nakai and Dakota traveling mercy to return home safe and sound. In Jesus' name. Amen."

Suddenly, Nakai's angular, handsome face appeared in her mind. When he gazed at her in the dream, his familiar deep brown eyes appeared black and hypnotic. His powerful arms had imprisoned her in a tight, possessive embrace.

Maybe, if the situation were different, she could see him as that special someone who would give her unequivocal love. Wait! Had she lost her mind and gone crazy? She did not understand her reaction to the dream; he had seduced her where no other man could. However, although he may look after her when required, Nakai acknowledged her as a friend, nothing more, nothing less. Miliya yawned, thrust her fingers in the snarled mass atop her head, and moved to the bathroom to perform her ablutions.

CHAPTER 12

"What is Bash's horse doing here?" Nakai demanded, his eyes narrowed.

Royce had picked him and Dakota up from the Pinesdale Depot and had stopped in front of the main house before securing the horses and buggy. He debated on what his response would be to his obvious, irritated brother.

Two weeks ago, the day Nakai and Dakota departed to Butte, Bash invited Miliya to dinner at NICOLE'S, an elegant French-American restaurant. The owner, Nicolette Anais, a woman of French--Negro ancestry, served cuisine from crepe suzettes to filet mignon. Frequently, in the following days, Bash called on Miliya. Yesterday, he had accompanied her to church, which started tongues to wagging. This morning they had gone horseback riding, and now they were inside having lunch.

"I'm waiting, Royce." Nakai raised his thick brow as he tapped his fingers on the seat.

Dakota jumped down from the buggy.

"Where is Miliya?" Nakai repeated the question.

Royce faced the dark frown on Nakai's face, mindful of the pulsating vein in his neck, a sure sign his patience had reached its limit.

"Miliya is inside eating lunch."

Nakai narrowed his eyes again and   in a menacing voice asked, "With Bash?"

"Yes," Royce said. He closed his eyes tight and waited for the explosive response.

"How often has he dined here?"

"The same day you left was the first day he visited." Royce grimaced. " And he hasn't missed a day since."

Nakai bounded from the buggy with a dark scowl on his face. He inhaled and exhaled a deep breath before he proceeded to the steps.

As they watched their retreating brother, Royce and Dakota simultaneously called out, "Nakai."

Glancing at Dakota, Royce said, "Go see about Wildman while I secure the buggy and horse. Let's hope Bash won't fly through the window while seated on a chair."

 Royce took the reins, giddied upped, and headed for the stables.

"Chicken!" Dakota hollered to Royce's back as he drove away.

Then, he started towards the house and hoped Nakai hadn't

rearranged the furnishings or changed Bash's appearance.

Nakai entered the house and placed his hat onto the hook of the hat rack. From the kitchen, the smell of Mama Louise's mouthwatering chicken assailed his nose. Laughter from the kitchen echoed through the house. Sounds, like they're enjoying each other's company, a little too much!

He had decided to woo Miliya before his trip to Butte. He also promised himself to control his anger and the jealousy that had reared its ugly head, thanks to his best friend. Yet how can he be jealous when she wasn't his? Nakai desired to know everything about her, from her favorite food to her favorite book. She once was a vision in his dreams, but now she had manifested into a woman. The blue-eyed-woman meant everything to him. Determined to take a chance and ready to activate his plan and feed his hunger, he strolled to the kitchen.

"Good afternoon, Miliya."

Immediately, all laughter and conversation ceased. Leaning down, Nakai placed a kiss on her cheek and whispered into her ear, "I missed you."

He straightened, nodded at a stunned Bash, and then slid his tall, impressive frame in the chair across from her.

Miliya appeared dazed.

Raising a brow, Nakai asked, "Miliya, are you feeling well?"

"I feel fine. Why do you ask?"

"Your face is flushed," Nakai said.

She touched her face with nervous fingers.

"Miliya looks like the sun-kissed her lovely face with color," Nakai answered for Miliya. His hypnotic eyes grabbed her attention.

"That could be." Bash smiled in agreement. "This morning, we went horseback riding. It was very sunny. That's where she was 'kissed by the sun'."

Nakai, his lips tight, shot his narrowed, dark eyes at Bash.

Miliya cleared her throat. "Nakai, Kensington Estates extends over acres of spacious land, lush green grass, and surrounded by majestic mountains. An absolute beautiful sight to behold."

"You're entitled to build your home on this land; if you so desire." Gazing at her, Nakai leaned back in the chair. Before she could comment, Bash piped in.

"That would be great if you built a home here, Miliya. That means you'd be near me for as long as life allows."

"Bash, we would be friends whether I built a home or not."

"I'm counting on it. Who knows what life has in store for us." He reached over and placed his large hand over hers and squeezed.

His remarks caused Miliya discomfort. She had just told him they'd be friends. Did he think their friendship could change into a romantic relationship? Not a chance. The dishes on the table had been set out, and Nakai had prepared a plate of fried chicken, potato salad, green beans, and cornbread. What would he think of her if he knew how she felt about him?

In that instant, he looked up. His inquiring eyes met hers, and she blushed. Did he hear her thoughts?

"How was your trip?" Bash turned to his friend.

"We delivered four stallions," Nakai replied.

"I'd like to purchase two Arabians," Bash said. "Anyone knowledgeable about prime horseflesh knows the Kensington Estate raises and owns superior horses."

"We're in the process of crossbreeding an Arabian and a Thoroughbred. The Arabian is an intelligent breed, with the inborn ability to get along with humans, making them easy to train. We have two purebreds ready for purchase," Nakai drawled.

"Let me know when I can come and look them over."

Nakai said, "Come by anytime. "

After a moment, Bash glanced at Miliya. "I expect to see you more often in the future."

Nakai ignored the twitch in his jaw muscle and asked, "Oh? Why is that?"

"I'll be coming over to check on Miliya and the K5."

Nakai addressed the woman across from him. "And you, Miliya, do you mind him coming over to see you?"

"I always have time for my friends. However, when I don't, I should hope they would understand," she said, aware that both men anticipated her answer. Miliya gazed at her friend's light brown eyes with intention.

"They do," Bash murmured, clearly disappointed at her response.

Nakai leaned back in the chair and rubbed the back of his neck. He unbuttoned the first three buttons of his shirt and rolled up the sleeves, revealing muscular brown arms. The shoulder-length hair flowed past his broad shoulders like black silk. His eyes closed. When they reopened a few seconds later, Miliya seized his gaze before lowering her eyes; she blushed again.

Nakai boosted from his chair and moved over to where Miliya sat. She drew in a sharp breath when Nakai leaned down and kissed her on the cheek. Pleased, he straightened his tall frame.

"I didn't realize how tired I was from my long train ride." He addressed Miliya. "I'm going upstairs to rest, and I will see you for dinner." He switched his eyes from her to Bash. "Did I hear you say you're leaving?"

Bash blinked. The expression on Nakai's face brooked no argument.

"Don't remember saying..." He stopped when his friend hurled an icy stare at him. "Miliya, I enjoyed your company today. We must do it again very soon."

Her eyes wide with disapproval at Nakai's rudeness, Miliya said, "Thank you, Bash. As always, I enjoyed our time together."

Bash reached for her hand and kissed her fingers. "Until we meet again."

"I'll see you to the door." Nakai offered, his eyes flashing fire.

Amused at the flashing fire in his friend's eyes, Bash proceeded out the door onto the porch, to the hitching post where he untied the reins and mounted the horse.

"Take care of my girl." Bash wiggled his brows.

With his arms crossed, Nakai said, "Always and forever." He believed tonight, her blushes, stolen glances, and continued declaration of friendship with Bash were signs she wanted more than what he and her shared now. Tonight, he would find out answers to all his concerns once and for all.

Miliya sat frozen in her seat, touching her cheek, where twice tonight Nakai had kissed her. If he knew how much his touch affected her, would it matter? She wasn't prepare for the shock waves coursing through her taut body. For the past week, thoughts of Nakai had monopolized her mind nonstop, day and night, leaving her with mixed emotions about the eldest Kensington brother. Gracious, how can she feel any way other than a sister towards Nakai? A still voice whispered, "He is not your biological brother."

No, he's not, but he sees me as a sister. Besides, he wouldn't be interested in a woman ten years his junior fantasizing about him! Then, why did he whisper, "I missed you," as though she meant more than a sister? She truly hoped Bash wouldn't seek more than friendship. Her heart had already singled out the man for her, his best friend!

Dakota breathed a sigh of relief. His friend's handsome features remained, as well as the furniture. His duty as a referee was over. He shut the door and headed to the kitchen. His stomach was growling!

Bash realized there was something between the pair, nothing tangible, at least not yet. He liked Miliya. She was a Christian (such as himself) personable, caring, and beautiful. He intended to pursue her. If Nakai doesn't step up and reveal his true feelings soon, he would go forward with his plan to claim the heart of Miliya Davis.

CHAPTER 13

Rolling her eyes around, Miliya laughed and said, "I'm full up to my eyeballs in your delicious deer stew." Miliya laughed, rolling her eyes around.

"You must have been mighty hungry, baby," Mama Louise shook her mixed gray hair. "Two full bowls disappeared into that slim tummy, along with a hunk of cornbread."

Nakai scrutinized the laughing woman sitting across from him. Her infectious laughter brought to remembrance the verse in Proverbs 17: 22, "A merry heart doeth good like a medicine," just as her presence was a soothing balm to his ravaged soul. After dinner, he intended to put his plan into action. A frisson of fear traveled through him. What if she didn't want an intimate relationship with him? Her refusal would crush his heart. His life would resume as it had for the past two years if his admission to pursue more than a sibling relationship had a negative impact on their friendship.

Miliya declined dessert. "If I eat one more morsel of food, I'll burst."

Nakai pushed his slice of apple pie aside and observed her in silent contemplation.

"Miliya, would you accompany me to the porch? I need to discuss a matter with you."

Her brows arched.

"Please?"

Miliya relented at his plea. "Yes." Her voice sounded small.

He stood from his seat and moved around the table to where she sat. She accepted his proffered arm as he led her to the porch. Five pairs of eyes followed them out the door.

On the porch, four cushioned rocking chairs sat inches apart. They each selected a rocker and settled back until they were comfortable. Seconds rolled by while the man and woman watched fragments of daylight dissipate in the blue sky. Nakai let out a sigh. He glanced over at Miliya. Her eyes closed as she rocked back and forth.

"Have you enjoyed your stay with us so far?" Nakai scanned her face. She faced him with a bewildered expression.

"Yes. I'm thankful God brought us together as a family. Since I've been here, I've experienced genuine love."

Nakai smiled. "In the two weeks you've been here has any man caught your fancy?"

Confused, she gazed at him as though he had three heads.

"Why are you asking me this?"

"Miliya, answer me." His voice raised.

"What if I did?" She glared at his thick, black brows, slashed across his darkened face. Nakai rubbed the back of his neck and sat up in the rocker.

"Nothing." His full lips tightened. *Lord, why can't I express my feelings to her without sounding like a madman?*

Miliya tilted her head and asked in a soft voice, "Nakai?"

"Yes."

"What did you want to talk to me about?" Their eyes met and lingered.

"I wanted to know if all is well with you and if there is anything, I can do to assure your comfort."

Coward! He dropped his head.

Miliya frowned. "By asking if I had my eye on someone?"

"Do you?"

"The truth?"

"Of course!"

"Yes. But he doesn't know. I'm younger by at least ten years. It's just a crush."

"Do I know him?" He croaked. *Relieved, the man didn't know of her attraction.*

"It's possible, but don't ask me his name. It's a crush. I'm sure it'll pass." She shrugged a shoulder.

"Of course. If you need to talk about this or any subject, I'll be here for you." The smile on his face never reached his eyes. Smiling, on the outside, he was seething on the inside. *Who is this man? Is he even worthy of her? Look at her; she is a picture of a virtuous woman. Lord, I need your guidance. What to do now?*

"Nakai, have you anyone you're attracted to?"

His lip quivered. Now it was his turn to confess.

"Well, there is someone, but she has her eye on another."

Miliya regarded him with eyes of compassion. "We are in the same predicament. Seems, we're both unlucky in love."

"You know, two years ago, I was in a relationship with a woman I planned to marry." Nakai glanced at her. "I'm sorry. You don't care about my romantic failures."

She pushed the rocker next to his. Her gentle touch stroked his arm. "If you could listen to my woes, I can listen to yours."

Moved by her sincerity, Nakai resumed where he left off.

"Two years ago, I asked the daughter of Jim Jensen, owner of the general store in town to marry me. Zelia appeared to be a loving woman, a Christian lady, or so I thought. I traveled to other cities for business. Zelia would pick me up at the station, and we would eat a meal, according to the time of day."

Miliya sat with a rapt expression.

"This particular day she didn't come. I hired a buggy and rode to her home at the edge of town. The thoughts of sickness and foul play filled my mind. When I arrived, I knocked on the door and found it unlocked. Her parents were at the store, so she should have been home. As I entered the house, the sounds of moaning were coming from the parlor. The door was ajar, so I pushed it open and received the shock of my life. Sitting on the sofa were my fiancée and a man with his hand rummaging around in her blouse. Something I never did. I gave her the utmost respect with my love." Pain-filled eyes looked at Miliya.

"What happened when they saw you?"

"I don't think they saw me. All I knew was I had to leave at that moment before I did something stupid."

"Is she still around?"

"No, thank God. That night, she ran off with him, a traveling salesman. According to her parents, she has been in three relationships since then."

Nakai leaned back in his rocker. "That is the end of my romantic liaisons." He stared at the moon.

"That is, until this lady you have a fancy for." Miliya reminded him.

"That's a crush… like yours."

She looked thoughtful. "Mine is a crush, but yours with some ingenuity could be a reality."

"How's that?" He frowned.

"You must let her know how you feel. You're not a novice concerning women and love."

Nakai held her eyes. "Do you think she would be receptive to me if I proposed a get-together to discuss the probability of a friendly relationship?"

"Is she a Christian?"

"Oh, yes. A woman that loves the Lord and is caring, virtuous, loving, beautiful, and has a wonderful sense of humor. These are just some of the attributes that attracted me."

"I have no doubt this woman sees you as an honorable and caring man," she grinned. "A little unpredictable sometime;, otherwise, these are admirable attributes any woman would consider for a friend or a husband," Miliya assured him. She gave him a mischievous smile. "Besides, you're so handsome!"

"Based on these qualities, would you have a relationship with me?" Piercing eyes drilled into her.

Miliya explored his rugged features. A crease marred her forehead.

Nakai waited with the patience of Job for her answer.

With her eyes fixed on him, Miliya leaned forward.

Several seconds, ticked by before Nakai could speak. He cupped her chin in his large hand and penetrated her inquisitive gaze with a look of tenderness.

"I thought you knew; you were my special lady!" Gazing in her eyes, he pressed a tender kiss on her lips "You are my blessing from God." Nakai released her chin, amused at the shocked expression on her beautiful face.

He rose from his seat and lowered his gaze. "How's that for unpredictable?"

Her eyes filled with humor as she lifted her face to him. "I…" Before she could finish her sentence, Nakai pulled her to her feet to stand in front of him. Soulful eyes drew her into his gaze.

"I'm curious. The man you have a crush on… is it me?" He proposed the blunt question and then braced himself for the reply. From the way she flinched and the darting of her almond-shaped eyes, he knew the answer, but he wanted her to say the word.

"Yes," she admitted.

Eyes brimming with gladness, Nakai promised. "Miliya Davis, I will pursue you until the day we marry. God help anyone who gets in the way. Agreed?"

The young woman conceded with no hesitation.

"Good." Without another word, he walked to the screen door, turned and extended his arm towards her.

"Miliya?"

She moved with the grace of a queen and took his hand.

"Nakai"

He had kept her up all night! Even missed breakfast too! A cheerful smile spread across her face. In her dreams, the formidable rancher declared her his special lady, a blessing from God.

Lord, thank you. You have blessed me with a loving family and an honorable man who wants to share his life with me.

A knock on the door broke into her reverie. "Miliya."

Falcon! She tossed aside the bedcovers, donned her robe, and dashed to the foyer. She released the lock and opened the door.

"Good morning, sis." He stepped into the room. His sharp eyes scanned her body from head to toe. He appeared relieved after his perusal. Today he dressed in a dark suit, white shirt, and black leather boots.

"Good morning, brother. You look very handsome." She moved into his outstretched arms. He gave her a tight squeeze before releasing his hold.

"How are you feeling?" Concern filled his gray eyes. "You weren't at breakfast, and Mama Louise, Royce, me, and anxious Nakai were a bit worried when you didn't show for breakfast."

"I'm sorry, I overslept. Please give everyone my apology." A rosy glow moved over her face.

"Everyone is concerned you may have overslept, everyone except Nakai."

Falcon rubbed behind his neck. "He asked me to check on you and was very adamant about it, I must say." Peering into her eyes, he asked, "Is there something I should know?"

She nibbled on her bottom lip, uncertain of her answer.

"Miliya, what is it?" Falcon wondered if his eldest brother was somehow involved.

"I was coming to you today to seek your advice about something that has been on my mind."

Her brother studied her flushed face, the incessant rubbing of her hands, all nervous actions. He took her hand and led her to the sofa.

"Sit." Falcon pointed to the cushion. Obediently Miliya settled herself on the seat. He joined her.

"Let's try this again. What is troubling you?"

"I care for someone." She rubbed her hands, moving back and forth.

"Who?"

She swallowed. "Your brother."

"Which brother?"

Miliya closed her eyes. Would what she was about to reveal cause a rift between him and Nakai? The brothers? No matter the consequences, she must be true to them and herself. Clearing her throat, she announced in a clear, confident voice. "Nakai."

A glance at Falcon piqued her curiosity. His expression never changed. Did he hear what she said?

"Remember last evening when he said Nakai had something to discuss with me?"

He nodded.

"It was about us."

"Would you enter a relationship with him?"

"As sure as there is a sun in the sky. I'd be the woman of his dreams because he is the man of mine."

"How does he feel about you?"

"He desires me as his future wife."

"About time!" Her brother slapped his knee.

She blinked. Twice. "You're not upset?" She was flabbergasted.

"No. We're not upset. Dakota, Royce, and Raven know too." Falcon was amused at the stunned look on his sister's face. "Before you came into our lives, Nakai had been having recurring dreams of a woman who had a hold on his life. As a doctor, I was alarmed about his health after viewing dark circles under his eyes from lack of sleep. He claimed he felt well, but I still watched for signs of extreme fatigue. For two weeks, Nakai had these visions until he met you. Miliya, you are the beautiful woman in his vision. Ever since, he had held back his true emotions."

A lone tear traveled down her face. She had considered Nakai as an angry, possessive man, changeable when most of the time he was fighting an inner battle to hide his true feelings for her.

"It saddens me that I caused the turmoil he had to battle daily." She dabbed at her tear.

"Most of the anger he expressed wasn't because he fought his affection towards you, but issues deep within he needed to resolve. Wipe these tears and give me your beautiful smile." He tweaked her nose. Her blue eyes twinkled, and her lips curved into a smile.

A loud banging on the door startled them. The siblings looked at each other.

"Nakai?" Miliya whispered.

"Better believe it." Falcon shook his head. "I forgot. He gave me five minutes to see about you. Guess times up!"

Falcon wandered over to the door and jerked it open. "We're not deaf!"

"Humph!" Nakai brushed past Falcon and stalked over to the sofa where Miliya sat. She was transfixed.

"Five minutes, big brother. The lady has to attend to her toilette." Falcon walked to the foyer to allow them privacy.

"Forgive me for banging on the door, but we were wondering why you missed breakfast. I asked Falcon to come over and see if there was a problem."

She loved his breathtaking smile. Miliya ran her fingers through the hair tossed about her head trying to make some semblance of her appearance. Giving up the task she responded to Nakai.

"I overslept. I'm sorry if I caused you all any unnecessary worry."

Nakai allowed his intense eyes to scan over Miliya from head to toe

"I am happy you are well. Since you missed breakfast, I'm inviting you to a picnic lunch with me. I'll ask Mama Louise to pack us a basket of goodies. Do you accept?"

"Yes. I'm famished."

"Good. I'll be by at noon, an hour and a half from now." He rose and reached for her hand, pulling her up to her five feet-nine-inch height.

"See you later." He leaned down and brushed his lips against her forehead. Grabbing her hand, they walked together to the door.

Falcon addressed his brother. "You were on your last minute."

"See you later, Miliya." He pecked her on the cheek and opened the door. As Nakai lingered, he held her hand.

"Ahem." The couple looked over at their brother. "I'm leaving, and so are you."

Squeezing her hand, Nakai brushed past a grinning Falcon.

CHAPTER 15

Sunday morning, Miliya and the Kensington brothers slipped into the second pew as Pastor Owens stepped up to the pulpit.

"We will have times in our lives when our loved ones mistreat us, and disparaging things might happen. But don't let pain and bitterness control you because they are the trappings of the devil. Instead, forgive! Bitterness settles deep into your heart, like a root. The scripture says in Hebrews 12:15, 'You mustn't allow any root of bitterness to spring up or trouble you, thereby many will be defiled or corrupted.' The more you hold on to these negative emotions, the deeper they settle within, infecting you and those around you. Dig up those deep-rooted hurts. Did you know the more you dwell on the hurt and pain, bitterness grows?"

The pastor looked up from his bible and smiled. "When I was a young man, about the age of twenty, a young woman broke my heart. I believed her to be a godly woman. Was I in for a rude awakening!

"We had courted for a year, fell in love, and got engaged. The day before our wedding, she came to me crying that she was pregnant by another man. Before coming to tell me, they married to save face with her parents and the community. I will admit she shocked me to the core of my being. I gave this woman love and respect, the entirety of our relationship. Bitterness became my friend, and pain accompanied me everywhere. Anger raged in me until it overflowed into my relationship with others. People avoided me like I had leprosy.

"My father knew fishing relaxed me, so one day, he told me to get my rod and go with him to the river behind our house. Several moments passed before he said, "Let it go, son. You're killing yourself inside and the relationships with people that love you with this anger and bitterness. Trust God. Trust him to bring you justice. Forgiveness is a choice. Cut these roots, let it go!

"And today I am telling you, per the scripture Ephesian 4: 31-32. 'Get rid of all bitterness, rage, and anger, brawling or slander, along with every form of malice. And be ye kind one to another, tenderhearted, forgiving one another, even as God for Christ's sake hath forgiven you.' My friends, as I close, forgive others, or your Lord will not forgive you.

"Allow love to guide you, not anger. Search your heart for any bitterness, deal with it, and forgive. Know that your Father will make all wrongs right. If you wondered what happened to that young lady, her husband left her after one month, she lost the child, and she became bitter. Long story short, she accepted Jesus as her Savior, and with the Lord's blessing, became my beloved wife." He looked down at his wife, sniffing and wiping her eyes with a handkerchief.

 The congregation stood, clapping shouting "hallelujah and amen." Their pastor's wife was one of the sweetest, gentlest, and compassionate woman in Pinesdale.

 "Hello cousin." Recognizing the masculine voice, the two young women turned around. Kayja received Nakai's peck on the cheek.

He moved over to Miliya and gave her the same. The redness on her face was the evidence Kayja needed to confirm her thoughts about their relationship.

"Nakai, will you take part?" My goodness, is he holding her hand?

"If Miliya takes part, so would I." He regarded the woman at his side.

"Great! If you think you'd recognize her basket, guess again?"

"What do you mean?" Nakai cocked his head and directed his gaze at his cousin.

"The ladies will line the baskets on the table, and the highest bidder will take that basket."

"Will I be able to see the contents? After all, the basket could be loaded with rocks."

Kayja looked at Miliya with raised brows.

"Good question. Yes."

"Each man can look at the contents, and then they can bid."

"We trust the ladies will not reveal the goodies in their baskets; that would not be fair." The couple nodded in unison.

"Well, here they are, holding hands," Bash sneered as he sauntered up to the trio.

"Mister King, what are you up to today?" Kayja smiled.

"Looking for a dinner invite. We bachelors who cook tire of our culinary expertise. Nothing like homemade cooking and desserts." Cinnamon brown eyes gazed at the woman standing next to his best friend.

Kayja tried to refocus his attention. "Today, you can bid on a basket full of homemade delicacies, contributed by the single ladies of the church."

"Are you one of those ladies?" Bash gazed at Miliya.

"I was thinking about it. Anything to support the church."

"Well, I'll be there. I pray I win your basket."

Kayja felt the heat from Nakai. The hard breathing, balled up fists, and clenched teeth announced his anger.

"If you still have teeth!" Nakai hissed. He released Miliya's hand.

Oh no! "Bash, come with me." Kayja pulled his arm. Both men glared at each other.

"I'm ready to go home, Nakai." Miliya grabbed his arm and tugged.

"Kayja." Nakai nodded and secured Miliya's hand. The pair walked across the yard oblivious of the questioning looks on the faces of the remaining congregation, including the other Kensington brothers.

Grinning, Bash asked, "You didn't want to go anywhere, did you?"

"Do you have a death wish?" Kayja shrieked.

"I'm not afraid of him. He wouldn't hurt me. We've been friends for too long. 'Sides, I was joshing him."

"Bash, friendship or no, I would think you would know better than to approach his woman as though he wasn't standing there. You know how he feels about her! Any other time, he would have severed your arms from your body, and you know that. Miliya's presence has a calming effect on him, and that is a blessing." Her arms flailed. Kayja was angry. They were family; she was very

protective of her family, especially Nakai! "Maybe, you're jealous," she accused.

"I'm sorry for my display —"

"Of jealousy?" Kayja finished.

"Yes. You are right. I know my friend is in love with Miliya, but then again, so am I. But all is fair in love and war. So, they say, but as you said, I favor my arms attached to my body. I've seen first-hand his protectiveness towards her, and I wouldn't want to be the object of his anger."

"I'll keep you in my prayers, Bash. Once you and Nakai talk, things will be the same as before if you are honest with him."

"I hope so." His less than enthusiastic response touched her. She tucked her arm in his and headed to where her husband stood talking with his friends.

Tonight, they would have a guest for dinner.

Bash scowled. His eyes watched the couple, followed by the brothers, stroll to their carriage. Kayja was right. He was jealous. In all his thirty-six years, he had never seen a woman with such beauty, integrity, and poise. The fact that his best friend told him he would take care of her should have been the end of it. But how do you turn off the profound feelings he had for Miliya? It will not be easy, but he must hide his feelings and keep his distance as much as possible. He knew if he ever had the chance to pursue her, he would. In the meantime, he would pray for deliverance from jealousy. As soon as possible, Bash would apologize to his friend for his disrespectful behavior.

Jake hid in the thick underbrush. Tsk. Tsk. Tsk. The blue-eyed beauty had two men vying for her attention. Enjoy her beauty now, gentlemen. Soon she won't be around.

The following week, Nakai and Miliya had two unexpected guests: Kayja and Bash. They arrived on separate days. Kayja wanted to go over the details of the basket outing. They were having coffee in the kitchen when Kayja suddenly asked, "Why didn't you tell me about you and Nakai? I thought we were friends." Miliya saw the hurt in Kayja's eyes and knew she had to tell the truth.

"Firstly, I want to say I didn't mean to hurt your feelings. My sentiments toward Nakai changed after the night Bash came over for dinner and asked to go out on the porch to watch the sunset with me. As we left, I heard growling sounds and chairs tossed to the floor. Bash hurried me out saying 'a wild dog got loose.'" Kayja tried to hide her amusement.

"But the furniture was intact and no dogs."

"Did you find out what was the noise you heard, the growling?"

"The comment Bash said about the wild dog made me think about dinner. When Bash asked to go on the porch with me, there was a low snarl coming from his side. Nakai sat next to him. I just put two and two together. It makes sense now since I know his feeling for me."

"From the moment I met you at the estate, I knew he was fond of you. More than what he was saying. Remember when he came in and hugged you?"

Miliya nodded.

"He held you as though he was starving, and you were a chicken leg. Then, when he whispered into your ear words for you only, I

knew then my cousin had affections for you." Tears ran down her face. She pulled out a lace handkerchief from her bag and dabbed her nose. "I'm such a blubbering romantic."

"You, the Kensington brothers, and Mama Louise knew how I felt before I did."

"How about Bash? Did he know?" Kayja asked.

"I don't think so."

"He is in love with you. Last Sunday, when you and Nakai left the church grounds, I told him about himself. He claimed he was joshing Nakai when the truth was he was jealous."

"Jealous?"

"He admitted it. I told him he'd better be glad my cousin didn't rip his arms from his body, approaching his woman like that."

"But he didn't," Miliya replied, defending Nakai.

"I know. You're like a shot of laudanum, calming, relaxing to him. You are his angel. Do you care for Nakai?"

The young woman thought but a second. "Truth is, I'm in love with him."

Kayja clapped her hands. "I know. He feels the same. It's in his eyes whenever he looks at you."

Miliya shook her head.. "We have known our feelings for each other only a few weeks. He couldn't love me, have affections maybe, but love is a strong word."

"Believe it or not, he would tell you himself and soon. Just one thing, you hurt him, and there'd be nowhere on God's green earth you could run and hide. I'd find you." She smiled sweetly. "Can I have some more coffee?"

Two days passed before Bash visited the Kensington Estate. He found Nakai leaning against the rail of the fenced-in paddock and watching Royce break in a mare. Bash handed the reins of his horse to one of the ranch hands, who led the animal to the barn.

"Morning, Bash," Nakai said without turning around.

"Morning, Nakai." Bash stood next to his friend and rested his arms on the fence.

Silence ensued as they watched the young man on the bucking horse jump around the enclosure.

"What brings you here?"

"I've come to apologize to you and Miliya." Bash focused his attention on Nakai.

The man didn't move an inch, but Bash was determined to make things right between them. Nakai pushed his Stetson back on his head and turned towards Bash. A frown creased his brow.

"Speak."

"I was ripped apart by your loving cousin, who told me I'm jealous of you and Miliya." He met his gaze. "She was right. I am." The other man remained silent.

"She is a beautiful lady with a demeanor that makes it easy to talk with her; she is the essence of everything I want in a woman."

Nakai's bronze features suggested no emotion.

"We've been friends for many years, and I don't want to lose my friendship with you over this. Please, forgive me." Bash held his breath.

Nakai gave a lopsided smile. "You're forgiven. But don't let it happen again, or I may have to gouge your eyes out." Bash paused at the vehement words.

"Kidding." Nakai patted his friend on his shoulder.

"Where's Miliya? I want to apologize to her as well."

Nakai lifted both brows. "Don't push it."

"Of course," Bash murmured. Nakai didn't trust him around her. He had no worries. His lady had eyes only for him.

"You might want to take a look at this stallion Royce is trying to break. He's a prime piece of horseflesh."

Thoughts filling his head, Bash returned his gaze to the corral. Nakai was changing, and he believed Miliya was the reason. He would always befriend the couple.

"When are you going to take care of that high yeller wench?"

"When I feel like it," Jake snarled.

"I paid you well to handle her demise as soon as possible. Get to it!"

"I don't like to be ordered round like a meager slave. Best watch your mouth, or you might get the same thing she does. You got me, weasel?"

Outraged, the heartless killer get on his horse and rode away. Jake

would be glad when the deed was done, so he could rid himself of the obstinate man.

After breakfast, Serenity found Nakai and a few men standing around the corral watching Royce break in a wild stallion. Laughter rang out when the horse bucked and unseated him. Shaking his head, Nakai hollered. "Save your kisses for your lady and not the ground!" His comment instigated more ribbing from the men.

Miliya wasn't interested in joining the rowdy group. She decided to pick flowers from Falcon's wildflower patches on the side of his house. The fragrant, colorful, plants would look pretty in her parlor. She gave Nakai a kiss and then rode off toward Falcon Crest. A warm, gentle breeze fingered her hair as clouds drifted across the sky. What a glorious day! Fifteen minutes later, she arrived at Falcon Crest and tethered Cloud to the post. As the young woman picked flowers, thoughts of Nakai invaded her mind. Imagine, Kayja thought Nakai was in love with her! Until the formidable Cheyenne said it, Miliya would embrace the fact he treated her like a queen and was always a gentleman.

Pop! She felt a ping hit her left shoulder. Looking around, she saw no one. When she gazed down at her shoulder, she saw blood seeping thru her white blouse. Someone had shot her! Adrenaline sharpened her awareness. She dropped the flowers and struggled to her feet. With the grace of God, she loosened the reins and mounted Cloud with a modicum of ease. Pain tore through her arm and the oozing blood soaked her sleeve. She had to get home.

"Cloud, take me home."

Father don't let me die alone. If I must, let me be in the arms of the man I love.

She struggled to focus through the oncoming haze threatening her sight. Just before her eyes closed, she saw Nakai, bareback on Lightning, charging towards her, his hair flying as he hollered her name. Royce followed behind with some of the ranch hands.

Behind them, Mama Louise drove a buggy. As soon as Nakai neared Cloud, he reached for the reins and pulled the horse to a stop. Dismounting, he ran to Miliya who, desperately tried to sit erect, but slumped over just as Nakai caught her in his arms. She was pale. Blood covered her left arm. Royce arrived and leaped from his horse. Fear and concern were etched on his face.

"Where is the buggy?" Nakai hollered. Tears filled his eyes.

"Mama Louise is here with the buggy. Let me help you..." Royce reached for Miliya.

"No! I have her." His steps slow, Nakai walked to the waiting buggy. With much care, he placed her onto the blankets and got in beside her.

"Mama Louise, are you able to drive back?" Royce asked the older woman.

 Tears were falling from her eyes. "I have to get my children back to the house." She turned the horse around and raced back to the house.

Falcon sat at his desk writing his notes for the day's cases when Jerry, a ranch hand from the estate, burst through the office door. The excited eighteen-year-old could hardly form a cohesive sentence. He tugged on Falcon's sleeve.

"Come, she's been shot. Please hurry!"

Falcon dropped his pen. Fear slammed into his gut.

"Who?"

"Miliya!"

"Where was she shot? How bad?" Falcon rushed about the office, gathered medicine and other items he would need, and put them in his medical bag.

"I don't know. But I saw blood on Nakai."

Falcon closed his eyes. Lord, heal my sister!

Grabbing his hat, he locked his office and followed Jerry to their mounts. Time was of the essence.

Across the street, a pair of brown eyes watched the doctor, and the ranch hand hightails it out of town. Satisfied, he smiled. The Kensington lady bled like a stuck pig from his bullet. Once she was dead, his job was over. The breed sure was a pretty thing, but money talked. He needed a drink of whiskey and while in the establishment, some female companionship. Turning, he pushed the swinging doors and entered the saloon.

Breathless with excitement, Deputy Collins barged through the Sheriff's Office door. "Sheriff Raven, your brother just left town in a big hurry. He was with Jerry Franks, you know one of the hands-on the estate," the slender man huffed, bending over, trying to catch his breath. "Someone's been shot."

Raven stood up. Fear coursing through his veins froze him to the spot.

"Who?"

"Miliya."

Raven raced out the door before Deputy Collins straightened up.

News of the shooting traveled through the town like a raging tornado. When Falcon rode up to the steps and slid from his horse, he gave the ranch hand the reins and climbed the six stairs two at a time. Horses and carriages of close friends and family cluttered the Kensington Estate courtyard.

Falcon bypassed the crowded parlor and ascended the steps to the bedrooms on the second floor. Waiting in the hallway were Kayja, Soma, Royce, and Dakota. Crying buckets, Mama Louise sat in a chair between the two women. She resembled a human waterfall. Before opening the door to the bedroom, Falcon bowed his head in greeting.

The sight before him wrenched him to the core. Nakai was kneeling and holding Miliya's hand. Weeping, he repeated her name, like a litany. Falcon walked to the bedside and gazed at the unconscious, pale face of his sister. Someone had ripped the left sleeve of her nightgown and wrapped a clean cloth about her blood soaked arm.

He removed the bloody cloth and examined the wound. Thank God! The bullet came through and exited. No structural or vascular damage and bleeding were at a minimum. Taking off his jacket, he laid it onto the arm of a chair and then he prayed. Lord, You are the Great Physician. I am but a man. Work through me what I need to do for my sister to restore her health. Touch my brother with your peace and restore his crushed heart, strengthen his spirit, for weeping may last for the night, but joy comes in the morning. In Jesus name. Amen.

He placed his hand on his brother's shoulder. Falcon knew he hadn't left his Miliya's side. "Nakai," he said softly.

His head rose, reddened eyes stared at Falcon. Nakai appeared dazed, a look Falcon had never seen on his brother's face. He was always fierce and confident. His love for Miliya spanned beyond the average definition of love; she was his soul mate.

"I will ask our brothers to escort you downstairs to get coffee."

"I love her, Falcon. She may not love me right now, but she does care for me. Nothing can happen to her, you hear, nothing!" He was frantic. Nakai jumped from his chair and grabbed Falcon by his shoulders.

The door opened, and the three Kensington brothers rushed in. With compassion in their eyes, Dakota and Raven subdued their upset brother.

"Royce, ask Mama Louise if she will make a pot of coffee." Falcon's eyes swept the room. "Nakai could use a cup, and I believe you all could use a break too."

"You may need help. I'll stay," Royce volunteered. He looked from the bed to Nakai. "I love them both. Please let me help!"

"Very well. Bring me a basin of hot water." Royce disappeared out of the room.

"Help her," Nakai whispered. Disoriented, he bent down, kissed her warm lips, and walked out of the room. Dakota and Raven followed.

Falcon stopped Raven. "Clear out the people, just family." His brother nodded, walked out of the room, and closed the door.

Twelve hours later, blinking to clear her vision, Miliya forced herself to open her eyes. The effort to sit up caused her pain. Exhausted, she dropped back down onto the pillow. Her right arm touched something warm. Startled, she looked down at the black-haired man sleeping on the edge of the pillow. Nakai. His warm hand slung over her stomach. She touched his head with gentle fingers. On

126

further perusal of the darkened room, another man slept slumped in a chair, his long legs stretched out in front of him.

Instinct told her it was Falcon. She grimaced at the sudden pain shooting through her left shoulder. Her memory was fuzzy, but this she remembered: someone had shot her. As she succumbed to the impending darkness, she lovingly laid a gentle hand on Nakai's head.

Sipping a cup of strong coffee, Royce asked, "Is Nakai still sleep?"

Last night, Falcon reported Miliya should be up within a week. Louise had cooked a celebratory breakfast the next morning for everyone on Kensington Estates. The hands had eaten and started their day while the two brothers had slaked their hunger and were enjoying a cup of coffee.

"Yes. I told him the bullet grazed the shoulder, and the bleeding had stopped. If the bandage stayed clean and dry, and no infection set in, she would recover in a week. But I think he'll be thrilled when he feels Miliya's hand on top of his head." Falcon was happy because that meant she had awakened during the night. The bleeding had stopped, but he had to keep an eye out for any temperature rise. The last thing she needed was a fever, a sure sign of an infection. He felt that God's healing hand was on her.

"Did the ladies get home all right last night?" Royce addressed Falcon.

"Luke and Kayja dropped Soma off at her parent's home."

"I wonder why Soma hasn't married?" Royce fingered his cup. "She moves with quiet grace."

"Maybe no one had approached her," the doctor said.

"How about you? Do you think she was attractive?" Royce eyed his brother.

"Any man would be proud to court a fine upstanding woman like her."

"A hah! And why haven't you?" Royce asked.

"I do not want to pursue Soma. For now, drop the discussion, little brother." He pushed his chair back from the table.

"I'm going upstairs to check on Nakai and Miliya." Falcon ignored the speculative look on Royce's face and mounted the stairs.

The sunlight peeking through the curtains illumined the room as Miliya opened her eyes.. Glancing down, her right hand rested on her stomach; Nakai had left, Falcon too. Her shoulder ached. She was awake, but she felt like she was in a dream. Someone had tried to kill her. Why? There had been no other human being in the area around the garden, so where was this person hiding? Who hated me that much to kill me? Unwanted moisture formed in her eyes. It could be anybody! She was on Kensington land, her home.

Humph! The shooter would not put fear into her heart. Nana always reminded her that God did not give her the spirit of fear, but love, peace, and a sound mind. She tried to sit up. Her tender shoulder throbbed and forced her back onto the pillows. The helplessness she felt was foreign to her body. The smallest thing, like getting up from the bed, hindered her. Her mouth felt like the hot sands of a desert. She reached over and grabbed the handle of the water pitcher on the stand next to her, thankful it was on her right side.

"What are you doing, young lady?" Falcon entered the room in two long strides, stood by the bedside, and gently removed the pitcher from her grasp.

"I could have poured myself a glass of water." She pouted.

"Not today. Most of your strength hasn't returned. Until it does, you're under the mercy of Louise and me." He shook the pitcher. "See, no water. You risked falling out of bed, or worse, breaking your right shoulder over an empty pitcher!"

"I'm sorry, Falcon. Please don't be angry." Her pleading voice caused him to sit down on the bed and regard her with loving eyes. He realized the impact this injury must have on her. With the pain came the emotional symptoms: nightmares, insomnia, and depression.

He would keep a close eye on her in the coming days for signs of fever and emotional distress.

"Miliya, the bullet grazed your left shoulder. The good news is it didn't damage any main arteries. I'm your doctor, and you need your mental and physical health to heal. The sooner, the better. You follow my instructions, and God would do the rest. How's that?" He placed his hand onto hers.

"Sounds good, doctor." The siblings looked towards the doorway.

"Nakai!" Miliya shouted as she threaded her fingers through the tousled mass about her head. Falcon mused. A gunshot perforated her shoulder, and she ponders over how she looks for her man. Women! Falcon rose from the bed and watched his brother rush over to Miliya, scanning her face with eyes that blazed love before possessing her hand. Falcon had never seen his brother happier. When Nakai had intercepted Miliya's horse, Royce told him he wouldn't let anyone touch her. The only time Nakai left her side was when Mama Louise bathed her and changed her clothing. He hoped now that he knew she was recuperating; he would get some sleep. Then, the shadows under his eyes would disappear.

"How do you feel? Are you in any pain?" Nakai kissed her forehead.

"I'm feeling better than I did yesterday, for sure. Healing will take its due course, one day at a time. If you are by my side, everything will be all right."

"Miliya, I'm going to ask you a question about yesterday. Are you up to it? Can I resume?" Nakai's sable eyes held hers.

"Anything to help."

Her brother stood aside but stayed in the room in case she needed medical supervision. Reliving the occurrence could sometimes cause any number of bad reactions.

"Where were you positioned picking the flowers? In the front, side, or behind the house?"

"On the side."

"That's good. Did you notice anything strange? See any strangers wandering around?"

"I saw no one," the answer was soft-spoken. Then she inhaled sharply.

"Nakai, there was a cigar smell. I remember saying to myself these flowers smell like a cigar. Don't like the detestable things. I'm glad you don't smoke." She wrinkled her nose.

"That's a lead. We can work with that. We'll ride out there to see if there are any tracks. Maybe we'll find a boot print, along with a discarded cigar butt."

Nakai studied her for a second. "You're beautiful." He gave her a brusque kiss on her lips.

She giggled. "Nothing is wrong with your eyes." She returned his tender look.

Falcon cleared his throat. "I'm going to see about your breakfast. Hot broth!"

"If you say so, brother." Her eyes caressed Nakai.

Right. She'll change her mind when she's looking down at a bowl of broth that resembled dishwater. He looked back at the couple, holding hands and whispering to each other. One day, he'd like to experience love with a special someone. There have been ladies in the past, but none that had captured his heart.

A knock on the door seized their attention. The door opened, and Raven, Dakota, and Royce entered.

"Well, big brother, Miliya's champion is here. Move over." Nakai rolled his eyes.

"Hello, Sis." Royce leaned over and pecked her on the cheek. The other two brothers followed Royce's lead.

"We came to check on you and see if you're feeling any better," Dakota said. "Your color has returned."

"Yeah, we're glad to see you up and still pretty as ever," Raven complimented.

"Thank you, gentlemen. I'm on the mend."

"Raven, Miliya remembered something that can help us in our search for the shooter," Nakai said.

All eyes settled on the woman leaning on their brother's shoulder. "I smelled cigar smoke."

Bobbing his head, Raven said, "Why don't we ride out and see what we can find in the surrounding bushes. There may be boot prints or cigar butts."

"It's a start. We would have checked the area yesterday, but we were more concerned about you. Let's go men and let the lady rest."

Raven walked over to Miliya and pecked her on the cheek again. He left the room.

"We'll be back later after we check this lead." Dakota kissed her on the forehead, followed by a peck on the cheek from Royce.

As Royce straightened up to leave, Nakai followed. "I appreciate your help in the care of Miliya. I was devastated, scared she may leave me, but you stepped right in. There have been times when I felt like snapping your head off, but I couldn't harm my baby brother. I love you and always will. Thank you."

Overwhelmed by his confession, Royce felt he needed to share.

"I love you and Miliya."

Nakai grabbed Royce into a bear hug.

"Nakai," he whispered. "I can't breathe."

Laughing, his eldest brother released him. "Sorry, little brother. At times, I don't know my strength."

"I do," Royce murmured and walked out of the room.

"I'm leaving, but I'll be back later." Nakai kissed Miliya's forehead, left the room, and quickly caught up to his brothers.

CHAPTER 16

The"K5" spread out around the side of Falcon's house and searched, inch by inch of the area for evidence someone had waited to shoot Miliya. Another question plaguing the brothers was how, where, and when did this person sneak onto their fenced-in land.

"Nakai, look at this." Royce stood near a thicket of thick chokeberry shrubs several feet away from where Miliya had been picking flowers. He held a cigar butt in his hand.

"There is another one," he said and pointed to the ground where another butt lay behind a tall bush.

As Raven watched his brother inspect the butt up close, he commented, "This person took his time watching her." Hunkering down, Nakai examined the ground and found that boot tracks led from behind the house.

"I would guess these tracks belong to a tall, heavyset man, judging by the deep impressions made in the dirt." The men surrounded him as he studied the tracks. Nakai ran his hand over his face.

"He approached from behind the house, tethered the horse on the bush. Then he sneaked around behind the bushes using their thickness to conceal his body, crouched here, and shot her." His voice cracked. The brothers exchanged a look of understanding.

Nakai released a frustrated sigh. "Royce select a few men and check the perimeter of the property for any signs of tampering. Follow any tracks and pathways leading from the house to the fence." Royce nodded his assent.

"Meanwhile, I'll be checking around town for any unfamiliar faces," Raven said. "Oh! One more thing. A reward would be an excellent incentive. People will bare their soul for a dollar."

"If you think that will help, I'll offer one thousand dollars," Nakai said.

The brothers whistled.

"She's worth more than that to me." He eyed each brother.

The thought she could have died had the bullet entered her body; instead of exiting stayed in the back of their minds.

Nakai's eyes darkened. "We must find this person. Next time he may finish the job." They agreed.

"Here's what we know," Raven began, "this man is tall, heavyset, and smokes cigars."

"Let's keep our leads to ourselves; tell no one," said Royce.

The five men mounted their horses and took off in their different directions.

In the following days, Nakai locked down Kensington Estate to implement the many changes he requested. The completed alterations satisfied him and the brothers. Three men kept the vigil of the grounds. Until further notice, access to the estate would be guarded by two able-bodied men stationed in a shack

fifty feet from the entrance of the property. Nakai gave the guards a list of approved names, and if a name was not on the list, they summoned Nakai. His utmost concern was Miliya's safety. Stone, a former Buffalo Soldier from the 9th Calvary, would accompany her whenever she left the property.

"Are the fences done?"

The brothers sat in Nakai's office discussing the numerous modifications that had been made to the grounds.

"We strung the last string of barbwire today." Royce slumped in the chair. "I never paid much attention to the height of the fence, but it's about five feet tall. If someone can get past barbwire, nailed on top and midway through the fence, they must be able to fly."

Dakota said, "Dad made sure the horses had enough space to frolic about without running anywhere near the fence."

Nakai looked over at Royce and studied him for a few minutes. "Dad and Mom would be proud of you, Royce. You've grown to be a responsible man."

"Trying to be like you, minus the crazies." He winked. Nakai shook his head. There was only one Royce!

"Well, before our older brother thinks about what you just said, I want to say something." Raven stared down at the floor.

"What is it?" Nakai asked.

"After our meeting, this morning, I decided to look around the guest house." He directed his green gaze into his eyes. "I found a cigar butt by the bedroom window."

"What?" Nakai jumped up and banged his fist on the table. Anger, fear, and rage burned in his eyes. He fell back onto the chair and closed his eyes.

"Same boot tracks leading off into a grove of trees near the southwest fence. The fence had been cut." Nakai didn't move or say anything. Raven met his brothers' concerned gazes.

"If there's any consolation, since all the changes have been made, whoever would have to be a ghost to get near Miliya again," Raven said with confidence.

"I pray so. If I have my way, anyone who tries to harm her again will never see the light of day," Nakai raised his face. "I promise you!"

"One thing for sure, she can't stay at the guesthouse, not while this fool is loose!" Dakota said.

"She's staying here," Nakai said.

"That is your logical conclusion for her safety, but what will the typical conclusion be when folks question her reputation for living in a house with a single man?" Falcon reasoned.

"Reputation?" Nakai yelled. "Her reputation means nothing if she's dead!"

"I understand your reasoning, but others won't."

"Do you trust me, Falcon, not to harm her in any way?" Still, dark eyes bore into him.

"Nakai, I trust you. But others will see you two as an unmarried couple living together. Miliya could be comatose, and it would not matter. You're not married."

"Did anyone think of asking Mama Louise? I'm sure she wouldn't mind staying here until this heathen is apprehended. Just my

thought on the matter," Royce suggested. Mama Louise lived a quarter of a mile from the estate. The brothers had offered Mama Louise the guesthouse after her husband Elias succumbed to the fever. She opted to stay in the home she had lived in for the past thirty years.

"I never thought people would think bad of Miliya other than she was sweet and virtuous," Dakota said. "People are narrow-minded. I don't want her hurt by malicious gossip that could ruin her reputation. I say ask Mama Louise."

Nakai looked around at each man. "Does everyone agree to ask Mama Louise to stay as long as needed?"

All heads nodded in unison. Nakai stood, went to the door, and opened it. He was startled to see Mama Louise standing there looking guilt-ridden.

"I thought you boys might want a snack." She pointed to a tray sitting on the floor. It was laden with a pitcher of lemonade, five glasses, and a dish of cookies, setting on the floor. Nakai looked from the tray on the floor back to Mama Louise. Crossing his arms in front of him and trying not to smile, he addressed her. "What's your answer?"

"I'm sorry. When I stopped in front of the door to open it, I overheard you yell about Miliya's reputation. That gentle young woman doesn't need another thing to worry about, at least, not from some narrow-minded windbags who know nothing about your and Miliya's respect for each other. I'd be glad to stay here for as long as you need me." Grateful, Nakai hugged her and planted a kiss on her cheek.

"Mercy, boy. Stop all that mushy stuff and pick up this tray and take it inside. I've got work to do." Nakai instantly obeyed.

A week had passed, and everyone had fallen into a daily routine at the estate. Three men checked the fence around the perimeter of the property three times a day for any damage. As proposed, there were two guards posted a hundred feet from the home entrance. As an extra precautionary step, every eight hours one of the men patrolled behind the estate.

This afternoon, Miliya was sitting on the porch reading the book of Psalms, when Stone approached her. The formidable man was assigned by Nakai as her bodyguard.

"Afternoon, Miss Miliya." She glanced up Stone and thought that the guard at the front entrance and him both had impressive physiques. They could well, strangle a horse if necessary.

"Afternoon, Stone," she replied. "May I help you?"

"I need to see Mr. Kensington."

Miliya told him to go into the house. Nodding, he entered the house.

Within seconds Stone returned with Nakai in tow, a scowl on his face.

"Wait here," he addressed Miliya. His long legs carried him the short distance to where the guards stood, their guns pointing at a man.

Oh, my goodness! Who was that? She watched the interaction between Nakai and the visitor. His angry voice echoed through the silence. Then, he was striding back to the house followed by a man who kept turning around and glancing at the gun Stone aimed at his back.

As they approached, she recognized the man as Ed Masters, her assailant from the church. The same weather-beaten hat he wore that ill-fated day, he held now in his hand. Nakai halted the men as he advanced onto the porch. Taking a deep breath, he pulled

a rocker next to Miliya and sat down before he leaned over and kissed her on the cheek.

"Good afternoon. I missed you this morning," Miliya said. "You didn't come down to breakfast. Are you feeling well?"

"I had coffee in my office. There is a mountain of paperwork that's been ignored this past week. But that is of no matter. You have a visitor."

"I see."

"Step up to the hitching post," Nakai instructed the man. "That's the closest you will get."

Not wanting to agitate Nakai any further Ed Masters followed instructions.

"Good afternoon, Miss Miliya." His voice wavered.

"Mr. Masters." The poor man so feared Nakai he wouldn't look his way.

"I come to apologize for that Sunday I buttonholed you. I was drunk. That's no reason for my behavior, other than I've been missing my wife. She's been dead for a year." Tears welled up in his eyes. "I tried to escape my loneliness through a bottle, and I realized that's not the answer. Me and my wife were believers for many years, but when she died, I lost my faith and blamed God for taking her. That incident with you had a sobering effect on me. I repented and asked for God's forgiveness, and now I ask for yours." He wiped the tears from his eyes.

Holding onto the rail, Miliya had raised herself and had descended the steps.

"Please, Miss Miliya, watch yourself." He started forward to help her, but the guard poked him in the back, a subtle reminder to stay put.

Nakai had caught up with Miliya before she reached the last step, six in all. Aware Nakai loomed close behind her, she reached for his hand. "Mr. Masters, I forgive you. Keep your faith in God; His love is unconditional. And, Mr. Masters," The humble man raised a tear-stained face towards her. "Abstain from liquor." She squeezed his hand.

"God bless you." Ed nodded at Nakai and, followed by the guard, retraced his steps back down the pathway to where he had tethered his horse.

"Don't do that again, Miliya!" Nakai thundered.

Tenderness shone from her eyes.

"Please?" he pleaded. "If he would have touched you..." Miliya tapped his arm and placed a finger over his lips, her touch halting his words.

With both arms, she hugged his waist and leaned her head against his broad chest. They stood there until Miliya couldn't stand the pain in her arm anymore.

She lifted her face to his. "I will do nothing foolish to cause you to worry about my safety. I am grateful to you and the brothers for all you have done to make certain I am safe. But Mr. Master's needed release from the guilt he carried, you understand?"

God, you have placed an angel in my life. Help me to be the man worthy of her.

"I understand you are a remarkable woman."

"That's right," she acquiesced.

Standing on the porch, Louise shook her salt and pepper head. "Y'all give the world a heap to talk about standing out there all hugged up. Lunch is ready." She went back inside the house mumbling. "Crazy children."

Ed Masters mounted his horse and rode off Kensington property. Whew! talking to the lady, Miliya, he feared for his life. Rumor around town was Nakai could eye a bear to bow with his piercing eyes. Ed thanked God he didn't get hold of him that Sunday. People who witnessed the scene said Nakai had blood in his eyes. Amidst the armed guard poking his back and Nakai glaring, he had asked for her forgiveness. When she accepted, he hightailed away from there. He pitied anyone who looked at or touched her the wrong way! God help them if they do and the Cheyenne caught them. Ed shuddered at the thought.

"Giddy up, Chester!" Let's get home!"

Sheriff Raven Kensington rummaged through the wanted posters on his desk to see if he recognized any of the faces walking around town.

One week had passed since the shooting, and there had been no further leads and no response to the reward money. Nakai had investigated every ranch hand, including the new hires, but there were no discrepancies. With all the safety measures applied, the estate resembled a fortress. Stone escorted Miliya everywhere she went other than on Kensington property. After a while, that had to be maddening for her. It's just a matter of time before they apprehend this lunatic. Then, everyone could breathe with a sense of freedom. He leaned back in his chair, and his eyes began to close. It had been a long day. When Deputy Collins returned from dinner, Raven was going home to get a good night's sleep. Tomorrow was another day.

One o'clock Saturday afternoon, Kayja had just removed a tray of hot brownies from the oven, when she heard a knock at the front door. Placing the tray atop the stove, she moved to the door.

"Surprise!" Miliya exclaimed when the door opened. Kayja recognized the stoic man standing behind her as Stone, the guard Nakai had assigned to accompany her friend.

"What a wonderful surprise." She embraced the young woman and nodded to Stone. Kayja led her guest to the parlor where they took a seat on the sofa while the quiet man with watchful eyes remained in the hallway.

"Excuse me, Stone," Kayja called, "Would you care for some brownies hot from the oven? Why don't you come into the kitchen, and I'll make you a plate."

"No, thank you, ma'am."

"You don't care for brownies?"

"I like brownies."

"Well, then come into the kitchen, and please call me Kayja. I'm family." She rose from her seat. "Miliya, I will bring a plate of brownies out for us. Do you want milk or lemonade?"

"Lemonade will be fine."

"Stone?"

"Coming." His long-legged strides placed him in the kitchen within seconds. Miliya smiled. Stone went with her everywhere, except the privy. She had become used to his presence. Whenever Nakai was available, he would accompany her, but today he had a business meeting.

Kayja returned with a plate of chocolate brownies, still warm from the oven, and two glasses of lemonade.

"I know a weakness Stone has," Kayja disclosed as she reached for one of the warm brownies.

Surprised, Miliya said, "I didn't think he had any."

"When I placed the plate of brownies in front of him, he chose one, and when he bit into it, his eyes rolled heavenwards."

She grinned. Miliya returned the smile. That was a picture she'd like to have seen. Seconds later, the man in the kitchen took that moment to appear in the parlor.

"Thank you ma'am for the brownies. Miss Miliya I'll be outside, checking on the horses." He nodded and started to leave when he was stopped by his employer's cousin.

"Stone?" Kayja pointed to his mouth. For a moment, the guard didn't understand her meaning, until Miliya whispered.

"Crumbs." She handed him a napkin. Unnerved, he dabbed the evidence of the six brownies he had consumed from his mouth. Thanking her, he nodded and exited the house.

"Is everything ready for tomorrow's basket bids?"

"Yes," Kayja replied. "Are you participating?"

"It's hard to say. If it were your cousin's decision, he would escort me home right after church services, but I'll participate. It should be fun."

-"Besides, I'll be surrounded by the K5, Stone, and a fleet of angels." They laughed.

"I understand. How has it been in the past two weeks?"

"Regarding my injury, I am grateful it wasn't life-threatening. My shoulder aches at times, but it's the nightmares that this man is chasing me with a gun and the anxiety that quivers in my stomach when I am suddenly startled by a noise. These things affect me the most." Blinking at the unwanted moisture accumulating in her eyes, Miliya shrugged in helplessness.

Kayja reached for her hand. "You are not alone. Yes, you have my cousins and the impressive Stone, but there is one who is within you and walks with you everywhere, willing day and night to comfort and love you, The Lord Jesus Christ. Hold steadfast onto your faith and trust God to work this situation out for you."

With tears running down her face too, Kayja hugged Miliya. When Stone entered the room, he noticed the teary-eyed women. Surmising, it must be a woman's thing, he turned around and walked outside.

Nakai and Royce Kensington walked into Sarah's Café to meet their brothers Raven, Dakota, and Falcon for lunch. Earlier that morning, a prospective buyer arrived from Denver to purchase three horses. After their meeting, they took him to the train depot.

The restaurant was the brothers' favorite for the best homecooked food and relaxed ambiance anywhere, including Nicoles. As always, the female customers displayed interest from expressions of longing to naughty comments. Nakai nodded, and Royce smiled, revealing twin dimples. From behind the counter, the waitress, carrying two menus, approached them..

"Gentlemen, your brothers are in the back room. Follow me."

The owner of Sarah's had had two large private rooms with the capacity to provide to fifty people for meetings or gatherings.

Royce and Nakai followed the waitress into the room, where the other three brothers were talking. She gave the menus to Nakai and Royce once they were seated. Within minutes they ordered, and a conversation began.

Sipping his coffee, Dakota asked, "How did your meeting go this morning?"

"Good. We sold three stallions. I am confident that Sasha, the Arabian, will be sold by the end of the month," Nakai said.

"Has Miliya been faring well?" Falcon asked. "I've been busy this week with several cases of fever, infections, and deliveries. Mark Lemmon's wife gave birth to their first boy. The poor man fainted with happiness." Falcon grinned.

"No wonder. He has five girls!" Royce said joining his brother's laughter. When the merriment subsided, Nakai responded to Falcon's question.

"Miliya's physical health is good, but I'm concerned about these nightmares she had been having."

Four sets of eyes pinned him with furrowed brows.

"Mama Louise sleeps in the bedroom next to hers, and Miliya woke her up three times last night, screaming." Nakai ran his hand down the back of his neck.

"You should have told me." Falcon's jaw tightened. This behavior was what he dreaded. He didn't believe in medication if he could avoid it. Prayer changed things.

"I'm sorry, brother. I meant to talk to you about the nightmares, but I missed you and Miliya at breakfast, and then I met with a client this morning."

"I'll come by later and talk to her," Falcon reassured him in a comforting voice. He didn't mean to sound brusque, but his sister's well-being was of utmost importance to him.

"Thanks." Relief colored Nakai's eyes.

Their food arrived, and all conversation ceased. After the meal, Dakota asked Raven if there were any new leads.

Raven shook his head. "Not a thing. I have my eyes open for anything strange, including newcomers in town. No one sticks out, at least, not yet."

"Maybe he left town," Nakai commented. Nothing had happened out of the ordinary since the added security measures.

 Four solemn pairs of eyes regarded Raven. His shoulders lifted in a shrug. Seconds passed before Royce spoke up. "How about those three men that kidnapped Miliya?"

The men's attention switched from Raven to Royce and then back to Raven, who was shaking his head.

"One day, the Lame Deer sheriff and a few of his men came and transported the kidnappers back to stand trial for murder. Soon after, I received a telegram from Sheriff Moody, stating they killed the men trying to escape en route to Lame Deer."

"I wondered who may have a grudge against Miliya. Those three had popped up in my head. How about Ed Masters? He wasn't too happy about the jolt between his legs," Royce scoffed.

"I can answer that with a definite no," Nakai said. "The other day, he came to apologize to Miliya and ask for her forgiveness. I escorted him to the bottom of the steps, and Stone poked a gun in his back. He spoke to her and left." A broad grin curved his lips.

"What's so funny?" Falcon raised his brows.

"After he had asked for forgiveness, he explained why he waylaid her and how that act changed him. Your sister paced herself down the steps, walked up to Ed, held his hand, and forgave him. On top of that, she told him to resist liquor."

Royce scratched his head. The other men shook their heads.

Grinning, Falcon said, "That's my sister!"

"How about Clyde, the bank teller?" Dakota asked.

"That young pup! He fears his own shadow." Nakai smirked.

"Stood up to you that night," Royce reminded him, aware of the dark eyes resting on his face.

"If it had not been for Miliya's soft touch on my arm, the young banker would be a dark spot on the wall," Nakai spat. His brother's devilish grin spread over his dimpled face.

"That's about all the people I know of that may have a beef against her," Raven concluded. "Let's all keep on our constant vigil for any unusual occurrences." He rose from the chair. "Got to get back to the office. Hope to see you at dinner." He opened the door, bumped into the waitress carrying dishes, and left the room.

Like he always said, money talks. A woman scorned was dangerous. The woman he bedded told him about her cousin, the waitress in Sarah's, who is knee-deep in love with the oldest Kensington who ignored her presence every time he ate there. A few dollars handed to her through the cousin provided him with the information he needed and the vengeance she desired. No leads. Get ready, Kensingtons, he was coming! Those barbwire fences made him think twice about tangling with them, and those apes with guns. Well, he had a plan. The waitress told her cousin about the church picnic tomorrow. He loved chicken. He hoped the blue-eyed woman was ready for his taste test.

CHAPTER 17

"Amen." Reverend Owens glanced around the full capacity church and closed his bible.

"Before the president of the Missionaries group gives us the details about the basket bidding, I ask you to join me in welcoming Sister Miliya back from an unfortunate mishap which led to her confinement over the weeks. She has asked me to convey her deepest gratitude for the love everyone has shown. Our God had touched her with his healing hand. Once again, she joins us in worship services. Praise the Lord. May you continue on the path of recovery, sister." His kind eyes regarded her as the congregation clapped and shouted, "Praise the Lord." They overwhelmed the young woman with their genuine compassion. Tears shimmered in her eyes.

She was appreciative to share the gospel with these loving, supportive people. A few seconds later, Kayja approached the front of the church.

"Good afternoon." She smiled at the returned salutation. "The details of the bidding are simple. We display each participant's basket on a table. You will see the contents. The highest bidder will picnic with the basket owner and enjoy the meal she prepared.

The women will supply the blankets. We will set tables up if you prefer that setting. All single people are eligible for bidding, and widows and widowers are included. Married couples have made donations. All monies will go towards the fund to purchase an organ. Let us all proceed to the grounds."

The Kensingtons joined the excited congregation leaving the church.

"I hope I pick your basket, Miliya. Just the aroma from your chicken will make me slap someone side the head." Royce smacked his lips.

Miliya laughed. "Long as it's not Nakai! He may slap back." They all laughed and elbowed the younger brother in his side.

Amused, Nakai slapped him on the back "Don't pout little brother!"

"Come on brother, if I win her basket, I'll give you the chicken. I only want to be near her." Nakai narrowed his eyes. "Understand?"

Royce gave him an affirmative shake of his head. "Is this what love does to a man? Makes him give up fried chicken?"

"Suppose you don't win her basket?" Royce asked, wary of the dark eyes, the knitted black brows, and the lethal look on his face.

"I'd hate to be him."

"Me too!" The young man shivered.

As they approached the tables, Nakai noticed the wives were setting out the food on the table while the husbands helped where needed. The participants lined their baskets on a table behind a curtain.

No one blinked at the tall, impressive Creole standing in the background, for everyone recognized the handsome man escorting Miliya around town. His eyes were intent on the azure-eyed woman in front of him. Out front, Kayja was about to give more instructions.

"Gentlemen, to be fair, all these baskets belong to the church. This way, you won't recognize any familiar basket. Beverages, lemonade, iced tea, and water are on each table. I will call each basket by its number to give you a chance to glance at the contents, but no touching. The lady, who is wearing the same number around her neck, will step out from the curtain and join the winner. We have food prepared for the men who don't win a basket. Now, will the first man step up?"

A young man wearing glasses approached the first basket. When Kayja removed the towel from the basket, the scent of chicken assailed his nose and his mouth watered. He saw the fried chicken, potato salad, gravy, green beans, cornbread, and a slice of pound cake. After the eighteen men reviewed the basket, she replaced the towel.

"How much do you bid, sir?" Kayja asked him.

"One dollar," he replied. The bids varied from one to two dollars until the last man bid two dollars and fifty cents. Loud clapping erupted around the crowd.

"We have a winner at two dollars and fifty cents." Kayja handed the basket to a handsome, strapping young man dressed in tan trousers and a dark jacket.

"Number one, please come to the front." A lovely young woman with hair pulled back into a ponytail and wearing a green dress with white trimming appeared, eager to see the owner of the basket. Her eyes widened, and with a visible intake of breath, she rewarded him with a tender grin.

Pleased at his choice, the bidder gathered the basket, took the young girl's hand, and they moved to the tables. Nakai smiled. Fourteen baskets were selected, and it left two. The bidding was between him and another man. Miliya folded her chicken wings. Nakai would select that basket.

"Gentlemen, let's check the basket."

Behind the curtain, Miliya and Christine waited expectantly. The young women had struck up a conversation while standing next to each other. Miliya had recognized her as the waitress from the restaurant Sarah's.

"They're bidding on number eleven; my basket," Christine said, nibbling on her bottom lip.

"I hope the man you care about selects your basket," Miliya said.

"Number eleven, come out!"

With a gasp, Christine grabbed the number from around her neck.

She turned to Miliya, "I never told you who he is."

"No, but it's not my concern," Miliya responded with a shrug.

"Not your concern? So, you think." Her laugh was harsh.

"What do you mean?" Miliya felt the hair on her neck stand up.

"Your almighty, Nakai! I've been serving him for two years at Sarah's, craving a hint he'd noticed me. But no. I wasn't good enough for the mighty Kensington."

"You show up with your honey-colored hair, light skin, and blue eyes and stole him from me! I prepared myself to hate you, but I find you're nice; you give me respect. He wanted me to stay clear of you, so he could shoot you. God, forgive me! That's why I can't let him!" Her eyes flitted about, finally settling on the wooded area.

"Christine, who is he?" Miliya tensed. Stone had overheard the conversation. His sharp eyes scanned the surrounding forest for the shooter.

The sun's reflection bounced off the rifle as a man stood up and aimed in their direction. Stone had no time to draw his gun. He lunged for Miliya, and they fell to the ground; his body pressed snug against her back.

A shot rang out, and Nakai froze; a frisson of fear slammed into his stomach. People dropped to the ground.

"Miliya! Miliya!" Nakai lifted the table and threw it to the side, flung the flap aside, and stumbled over a body. God, no! Upon closer scrutiny, he saw it was the waitress from Sarah's. He'd just seen her two days ago!

"Nakai," a soft voice whispered. He tilted his head and saw Miliya walking toward him, tears streaming down her flushed skin. He rushed to his lady and held her in a tight embrace.

"Stone saved my life. He knocked me to the ground and covered me with his body." Standing nearby, and observed the pair.

"Stone, thank you," Nakai said, his voice raw with emotion.

"I saw the shooter," he replied. "However, protecting Miss Miliya was my main objective. I didn't have time to pursue him."

"I understand. Join my brothers and me at the house. I'm taking her home." Nakai looked down at the honey blonde head resting on his chest.

"Sir, if you don't mind, I will accompany you. There was a madman out there." Without another word, he strolled toward the parked buggies.

"Nakai, what happened? Is Miliya all right?" Raven ran to the couple.

"The shooter came back," Furious, Nakai said. "Raven, he shot the waitress from Sarah's." His brother hunkered down to the lifeless body of the young woman lying on the ground. .

Raven was livid. "We have to find this savage!"

"Stone has information that you can use. Come by the house when your business here is finished. I'm taking her home."

"Miliya!" The worried voice of Falcon resonated through the bevy of people. The two brothers watched as he pushed through the crowd until he was standing in front of Nakai who was embracing his sister.

"Miliya?" She pulled away from Nakai and reached for Falcon.

"Why doesn't he leave her alone?" Falcon cried out in anguish.

At that moment, Stone pulled up in the carriage.

"Brother let's take Miliya home," Nakai said. "She's had enough for the day."

Falcon helped his sister onto the seat. Nakai jumped up next to her, and Falcon sat on her other side.

"I'll bring your horse, Falcon," Royce offered.

He and Dakota had just walked up to the scene. "We'll stick around and see if Raven will need any help."

"See you at the house," replied Falcon. The carriage and the guard on the black stallion disappeared down the dirt road.

The stupid girl! All she had to do was get the woman alone so he could shoot her. You can't find reliable help these days. Jake picked up the bottle of whiskey and poured a full glass. Bringing the glass to his lips, he downed the liquor in one gulp and then refilled the glass. That walking mountain, her shadow, saw him; he had an unobstructed view. He could be trouble.

This job was becoming complicated. He must deal with a hysterical whore, who hadn't stopped crying because the girl he shot was her cousin. She may need convincing to keep her trap shut! He downed the whiskey, wiped his mouth, and threw the glass against the wall.

Since the guard got a look at him, he would stay in the room until he could think of another plan. He couldn't wait to kill Miss Miliya so he could get out of this one-horse town.

Back at the estates, Nakai paced back and forth in the parlor, mumbling, his hands balled up in fists. The watchful eyes of his brothers followed his striding while thoughts of their own tumbled about in their heads. Stone observed the men with serene eyes.

When Nakai, Falcon, Miliya, and Stone arrived at the estate, Mama Louise had helped the trembling young woman to her room. Soon after, Raven and Dakota walked in, and the discussion about the shooting began.

"Stone, Nakai mentioned you have information," Raven said.

"Yes. The young woman carried on a conversation with Miss Miliya during the bidding. She was obsessed with Mr. Kensington."

"Call me, Nakai."

Nodding, Stone resumed. "This man had approached her to get information about Miss Miliya's case and to position her to get shot, but she changed her mind saying, 'You treat me with respect, and that is why I can't let him shoot you!' At once, I scanned the forest and noticed a man standing with a rifle in his hand, aiming in Miliya's direction. My immediate response was to protect her, so I pushed her to the ground, just as the shot rang out, hitting the other woman."

No one spoke. The enormity of what was said affected each man to the core.

"Describe him," Raven said.

"He was a brown-skinned, tall, heavyset man dressed in black. When I could stand up, he had hopped on a brown horse with a white spot on his right flank, heading towards town."

"Can you think of anything else, Stone?" Nakai asked.

"That is all, sir," he said. "I want this man caught and brought to justice."

"Thank you for your alertness and your loyalty to Miliya. You saved her life and mine."

"Miss Miliya is a woman who treats others with respect and warmth. I will do all I can to safeguard her from any harm," the imposing man said vehemently.

Nakai nodded his approval. His decision to hire the ex-buffalo soldier had been the right one These men served their country with courage, bravery, and discipline.

"I will send my deputy to search for tracks." Raven glanced around the room at the grim expressions.

"Do you need any help?" Stone asked and rose from his seat.

"No, but thanks. He knows you've seen him I don't want you out there in full view. It would be dangerous." Understanding Raven's logic, Stone nodded.

"We'll be okay, Raven. If you find out anything pertinent, let us know," Nakai said. His brother nodded, crossed the room to the front door, and closed it behind him.

 "Nakai, I will return to my post. Do you need me for anything else?" Stone inquired.

"No."

"I'm going upstairs to check on Miliya." Falcon excused himself and moved to the stairs.

"All right. I'll check around the corral. See you at dinner." Dakota said.

"That we should be saved from our enemies and from the hand of all that hate us."

Miliya read Luke 1:71 in quiet deliberation. This scripture applied to her situation. In the past weeks, someone had tried twice to kill her. There was no rational reason anyone would want to harm her. "Lord, I don't understand this situation I am in, but I know you are omnipresent, all-knowing. I trust you, Lord, to work things out for the good so you receive the glory. I rest in your word, mindful that your word will not return void but will accomplish what you desire and achieve the purpose for which you sent it. Amen."

She placed the Bible onto the bedside table. With all the excitement this afternoon, she felt fatigued and would take a nap before dinner. As soon as her head hit the pillow, her eyes closed, and sleep took control.

The next day Miliya stood at the corral fence, peeking through the slots. Royce dismounted the horse and gave the reins to Jerry. The young man led the animal to the barn to receive a rubdown.

"I've been working on this beauty for a week. It's about time she surrendered to the Kensington charm," he laughed, emphasizing the twin dents on his tan face.

"Is this a thoroughbred?"

"Yes, ma'am. Nakai had a rancher that wants to buy her. That's why I've been training all week. She is finally ready to accept a rider."

"Speaking of the Kensington charm, is there a special young woman in your life?"

A faraway look appeared in Royce's eyes and then, in a blink, disappeared.

"No one special." His smile did not reach his eyes.

"I'm surprised," Miliya said, "You are a Christian, easy-going, handsome, and intelligent. What woman wouldn't want you?"

He shrugged. "God has someone for me. She just hasn't come along yet."

Miliya observed Royce. Someone special had touched his heart, but he was not revealing her identity. As they approached the estate, someone was trying to get past the guards. A shrill scream sounded. It was a woman . She jumped at Stone, and he grabbed her arms.

When Miliya and Royce reached the steps, Nakai appeared on the porch. A frown creased his forehead. Descending the steps, he walked up to Miliya and kissed her on the cheek.

"You're looking radiant, Miliya," Nakai complimented. A louder scream reverberated in the air. Royce sent Nakai a meaningful glance.

"There's a problem I need to handle. I'll be back." She watched his long stride descend the path.

Miliya asked, "Who is that woman?"

Hesitant to speak Royce gazed at her for a moment before he took a deep breath and said, "Zelia."

Nakai, his piercing eyes narrowed, approached the three people.,

"Bow down, boys, King Nakai is here!" The woman's eyes sparkled with anger. "Order this henchman to release my arms! I'm harmless," the woman sneered.

Nakai nodded to Stone, and he released her arms.

"Although. they could park their shoes under my bed anytime." She winked at the men. Their emotionless expressions never changed.

"Zelia, why are you here?" Nakai had thought her callous and raunchy behavior would disgust him, but he only felt pity.

Of medium height, she was wearing a low-cut purple dress, which offered a peek at her assets. The thick black hair he used to admire was curled into the latest fashion. What had happened to the young woman he had fallen in love with?

"How can you ask that?" Her brows drew together. "I missed you and thought..."

"We could resume where we left off?" Nakai finished her sentence. a sneer on his face.

"Why, yes," she said and reached for his hand. When he stepped back, she frowned.

"Gentlemen, please give us a few seconds of privacy," Nakai requested. Stone and Abraham walked a few feet away, far enough for privacy but close enough if their boss needed them.

"Look, Zelia," Nakai began, "two years ago, you left me for another man and ripped my heart to pieces. I will admit, my thoughts of you were not of love; but murder. However, with time and a woman who accepts me for who I am, I can now say to you, without any hate in my heart, I forgive you."

"Forgive me?" she whispered.

He smiled. "Yes. God loves us and wants us to love each other, to be kind and compassionate towards each other: to forgive no matter the offense."

Glancing down at her dress, Zelia said, "I came here to seduce you, but now I'm ashamed." Tears shimmered in her eyes. "I allowed a man to sway me with his promise to give me instant wealth, but he lied and ruined my life."

Nakai shook his head. "Zelia, I don't understand. I'm financially secure, yet you left me. I would have given you the world."

"Lies I believed. He gave me a diamond ring, he had a pocket full of money, and he told me of a mansion bigger than yours, and that if I went with him, I would be the lady of the house with servants." She gave a harsh laugh. "What did I get? A run-down shack. He sold the diamond to support us and left when the money ran out. Pride told me to use what attributes God gave me to survive, and that is what I did." She looked at Nakai with tears falling down her face. "No man has ever treated me with the love and respect you showed

me. I apologize to you for any pain I caused. Hope this woman in your life returns the love and esteem you give from your heart."

She reached up and ran her hand down his cheek. How could he speak of love and compassion to her after she threw his love back into his face? Yet he stood there in forgiveness. With her head held high, she walked over to the buggy and stopped where the two guards stood. Stone assisted her onto the buggy, and she drove away.

Two days later, Miliya and Nakai sat on the porch talking, enjoying the solitude and drinking iced tea.

"I haven't brought the subject up about the angry woman at the gate," Miliya said in a soft-toned voice, "but I am now."

For a moment, he stared out at the mountains in the far distance and thought back to that day. When he had returned to the house, Miliya was inside mending one of his shirts.

"Miliya?"

She looked up from her sewing. "Yes, Nakai."

"I have solved the problem."

"When you are ready, tell me about it." She had picked up her needle and resumed sewing.

Affected by the encounters he had with both women that day, he had nodded and left the room,

He turned his attention to Miliya. "The woman was Zelia."

She crossed her ankles in front of her. "I know. Royce told me. I assume you talked."

"Yes. I did something I didn't think I would be capable of after two years." She glanced over at him.

"Want to know what it was?"

Clenching her hands into fists, her brows rose. "I sure do."

"I forgave her."

She gasped. His announcement shocked her. He gave her the details of what had occurred.

"She apologized to me. I feel good."

"So, did you have any feelings?"

"Any feelings?" Nakai looked baffled.

"Yes, feelings of love."

His dark eyes widened. Love? The only woman he had feelings for was sitting beside him, didn't she know that yet? Should he tell her so? She wasn't a mind reader!

But it was too early in their relationship to tell her, or she might think he was rushing her into committing when she wasn't ready. No, he'll wait for her to tell him her feelings.

"I felt pity. But the feelings of the love I had for her are not here." He splayed his hand over his heart.   Miliya heaved a sigh.

"Is there something bothering you, Miliya?"

"I am happy you have forgiven Zelia. Now you're both free. You from anger and bitterness. and it releases her from any hidden guilt she may have had." Her blue eyes lifted and searched his. "Are you happy?"

He stood up, pulled her to her feet, and hugged her in a tight embrace. "You make me happy."

Content, with her head resting on his chest, the two stood there until Louise called them to come in the house, all the while mumbling "crazy children."

"Listen, man, I gotta get out of town. The sheriff posted a thousand-dollar reward for any information on the Kensington woman's shooting. I knew that the bodyguard saw me. I sold my horse to a drifter last night. The saloon whore cried a river because I killed her cousin. , I shot the girl by mistake. The little waitress should have moved out of the way. The whore threatened to expose me, and I don't want to hurt her, but I would to save my skin. You, little weasel, find me a horse and a place to stay out of this town." Jake snarled.

The quiet man hated the demanding ruffian, but he despised Nakai Kensington more! If the blue-eyed woman accepted him, she would live, if not she would die! If he couldn't have her, no man would!

"At midnight, go to the edge of town, there will be a horse packed with food to last for a week along with directions to an abandoned trapper's cabin. You have no longer than a week to get this done." Jake's employer left the meeting place and mounted his horse. Before leaving, he reached for a handkerchief in his jacket pocket, covered his irritated nose, and sneezed. His sinuses react to the hooligan's cigar smoke every time they met. He couldn't wait till this was over.

Falcon locked the office. Office hours had ended when someone bumped into him. A bag of groceries fell to the ground and scattered its contents over the sidewalk. He squatted down to help, and when he looked up, he recognized the flushed expression on the mocha face belonging to Soma Winters. Long black lashes fanned her cheeks, while thick, black hair, loosened from the confines of a light green ribbon formed a dark curtain about her slender shoulders.

"Soma, I'm sorry. I didn't see you," Falcon said as he picked up a can of beans. "I didn't hurt you, did I?"

She nodded. "I bumped into you, and I am sorry. The bags covered my view."

After he retrieved the last item, Falcon asked Soma if he could drive her home.

"I can walk. It's not far, just at the end of the street."

"I am on my way home, and I'll give you a ride. Is that all right with you?"

The young woman averted his eyes. He was a handsome man, but so was Royce. She smiled at the thought of the young man with deep dimples and hazel eyes. If only….

"Yes, I'd like a ride."

Falcon placed the bags into the back seat of the carriage, helped Soma unto the front seat, and climbed in next to her. He secured the reins and yelled, "Giddy up," and they were off.

Royce left the feed store in time to see his brother help Soma onto his buggy. Falcon must have taken his advice and approached Soma. He wished he had kept his mouth shut. That should be him

in that carriage. Well, no use crying over spilled milk, big brother won! The young man felt like a horse had trampled him.

Falcon drove home thinking Soma Winters was an intelligent young woman. Once she overcame her shyness, she had a good sense of humor. She would be an excellent match for Royce, except his brother thinks Soma would be right for him! Falcon liked the young woman, but not as his mate for life. Besides, she revealed no interest in him. He was at the age he wanted a wife and children. He prayed for a perfect and divine mate, someone with the same beliefs, morals, and values. One day she would arrive, and he would be waiting.

CHAPTER 18

"Nakai, I saw Bash today at the bank. He arrived home from a business trip in Denver yesterday. My new stove hadn't arrived or else he could come to my place. Since this is your home, is it okay to invite him to dinner?" Dakota asked Nakai after breakfast.

His brother looked up from the Pinesdale Gazette. "Sure, why not?"

Dakota took a sip of the strong black brew. He placed the cup on the table and directed his gaze to Nakai. "Good to hear. He'll be here tonight."

The oldest brother returned his gaze and shrugged his shoulders.

"Will everyone be able to make it?" Dakota glanced at his brothers. They answered the question with a unanimous yes.

"Are you telling Mama Louise?" Nakai asked as he laid the paper on the table. She always prepared her menu for the week and welcomed no additions.

"Ask me what?" Mama Louise walked into the room. "Heard my name." She stood tapping her foot. "Well?" Her brows lifted.

Giving her a lopsided grin, Dakota broke the silence. "I invited Bash to dinner tonight. Is that okay with you, ma'am? You know how he loves your cooking, craves your chicken..."

"All right! Stop! Dakota, it's fine because I am in a good mood. In the future, ask me first. I have prepared my menu for the week. When having company, I cook something special."

Nakai tried to hide his grin. Underneath that gruffness, Mama Louise was a gracious person. If possible, she'd feed everyone on the planet.

"I told him to come at 6: 00 p.m. Is that a suitable time?" Dakota asked.

"As good a time as any." Looking around the table at each man, Mama Louise put her hands on her hips. "Finished? Get going. I have work to do."

Chairs scraped the wooden mahogany floor as the men fled the room, leaving behind Mama Louise laughing. How she loved those brothers!

Standing at the bedroom window, Miliya watched the five Kensington brothers scatter in different directions. They favored naughty young boys running to escape punishment. Out of the corner of her eye, she saw Nakai, his black hair hovering around his broad shoulders, striding down the pathway towards Stone. Judging by his casual dress of denim pants, a white shirt, and a black vest, she surmised he didn't have a business meeting, She watched him and the two guards, Stone and Abraham, share a laugh. It did her heart good to see him free from the emotional trials he had experienced because of the two attempts on her life. Miliya was thankful to God for protecting her and those she loved. He gave her his peace, which enabled her to rest in the plan He has

for her life. Moments later, she sat eating breakfast and laughing at Louise tell how she ran the boys out of the house.

"Mama Louise, you have outdone yourself! They should outlaw this meal!" Bash rubbed his stomach. "I'm stuffed!"

The matron shook her head in pity. "That's too bad. Guess the rest of you will have a second, maybe the third piece of apple pie, since 'I'm stuffed' cannot eat his share." Glancing at Bash, Mama Louise placed the pie onto the table.

Bash sat erect. "I'm more than sure I can squeeze in a piece of your savory apple."

"What a glutton you are. You're not getting my share!" Royce declared.

"All right, boys, everyone can have seconds, thirds too. I made two pies."

"Yes!" Royce jumped up and kissed the surprised woman on the cheek. Apple pie was one of his favorites. In fact, most desserts were!

After dinner, the men discussed the prices of feed, training horses, and current events, and Miliya helped the older woman clean the kitchen.

"It's been a few weeks since Bash has visited us. He looks good," Mama Louise commented.

"Yes, he looks like he's been doing all right. Dakota told him about my unpleasant incident, and he inquired about my wellbeing. That is why he brought me a box of chocolates and the vase with assorted wildflowers on the dining room table."

"I heard him tell Nakai he was in Denver on business and had visited his brother while he was there," Miliya said as she dried the plate in her hand with a dishtowel.

"Oh, that would be Tyler, the oldest. He owns a cattle ranch, a mighty large one, so they say."

"There are more siblings?"

"Yes, Marla. She's the youngest. Last year, she married Thomas Parks, and they live here in Pinesdale."

"Bash is a personable, handsome man. Why do you think he's not married?"

"You can ask that of the brothers too," the older woman retorted. "They're all convinced that their special woman hadn't entered their lives yet, that is, except your Nakai. I haven't seen him this taken with a woman, including Zelia." She shuddered.

"It will shock you when I tell you this, but Zelia came here and demanded to talk to Nakai."

Mama Louise gasped. "The nerve! What was her purpose?"

"To seduce him," Miliya whispered.

The older woman gasped again and held her hands over her mouth. Tears glistened like diamonds in her eyes. "Why doesn't she leave my boy alone?"

Miliya walked over to Louise and embraced her.

"Let's sit." The two women sat at the table. Unbelief radiated from the older woman's face.

"Nakai was obedient to God and forgave Zelia of any pain she inflicted on him. The pain, bitterness, and anger living in his spirit dissolved. He needed his joy, his life back," Miliya explained.

Louise wiped her wet eyes and looked at the young woman seated across from her. "Did he forgive her deceit as well?"

"Yes. He confessed it wasn't easy, but to have peace in his life; he forgave her."

"God sent you into my boy's life. He is more relaxed, and you are the reason." The matriarch rose and walked over to where the young woman sat and gave her one of her famous bear hugs.

When Mama Louise released her hold, the young woman sighed with relief. She was breathless. The widow could have been a successful wrestler.

"Sounds quiet in the parlor. Let's peek in and see what they're doing," Miliya whispered.

The closer the women neared the room, a cacophony of snorts, groans, and wheezing resonated in the room. They stood by the parlor entrance and tried to hide their amusement. All six men slept legs sprawled out in front of their respected seats. They noticed Nakai, content, had stretched his longs legs on the well-used ottoman.

"It was the second pie that did them in," Miliya whispered.

Laughing, the two women returned to the kitchen,

White puffy clouds drifted across a sunny, blue sky. It was an enjoyable day to go horseback riding.

"Miliya, I never knew you could ride a horse bareback," Nakai exclaimed as they sat on their mounts by the corrals.

The couple had gone riding among the vast Kensington acres after breakfast. Nakai embraced his Cheyenne heritage and rode without a saddle, enjoying the freedom it gave him. Thinking his companion was familiar with the conventional way, most women sat on a saddle, he was most surprised to see she rode bareback. However, her emerald green split skirt and a white blouse, tall riding boots, and a hat were conventional.

"My grandfather taught me how to ride each way: using a saddle and bareback. Back home, whenever there was a race, I always won. Most men are sore losers when beaten by a woman." She threw him a wide grin.

"Is that so?" Nakai asked. His left brow rose. "You win every time, you say?"

"Hey, you two, how was your ride?" Holding a lariat in his hand, Royce sauntered over to them .

"Miss Miliya appears to be an accomplished rider and had won every race she had entered in her hometown. she wins every time. Imagine that?"

"That's right. Every time." Her blue eyes intensified.

"Do say! Prove it!" Nakai challenged.

"How?"

Rubbing his chin, he pretended to be in deep thought. "Race me from the corrals to the gate entrance and back."

"Bareback, Miliya? That's a good distance from here, almost half a mile." Royce scratched his head. "Did you exaggerate trying to impress Nakai?"

The muscles in her face tightened.

"I mean, as an Indian, my brother has been riding bareback since the day he could walk, an inherent trait. Therefore, he has beaten everyone around here."

She smirked and tossed her hair behind her shoulder. "I don't impress easily, nor do I fear the unknown."

She was well-acquainted with the way most men thought. They didn't know the survival techniques, including riding bareback, taught to her by Grandpa Peter and the family friend, Mary Fields, known as the legendary Stagecoach Mary. She toted and used a gun with the skill of a professional gunslinger. As a favor to her grandfather, she taught Miliya how to shoot and handle a firearm.

"Nakai," Miliya turned her attention to Nakai, "what is the prize for the winner?"

Several men had gathered around listening to the exchange between the three people.

Grinning at his men, Nakai said, "Ladies first. I'll leave the prize up to you for the winner." Since he knew he would win, he hoped to name the loser's prize.

"The winner will do their favorite thing, such as I like to sew. When I win," she said, gazing at her opponent, "you will escort me to the Ladies Sewing Guild until we finish for the day. Also, take me to Nicoles every Friday evening for two weeks. I love their fried fish."

Nakai grimaced.

"So, Mr. Kensington, is that agreeable?"

Amused, Nakai replied, "Yes." After thinking for a moment, he said, "Now, here are my loser's rewards. You get to shine my boots, prepare my meals, and attend to any sewing repairs needed for a week."

He gestured to a ranch hand who rushed over to him, his head bobbing as Nakai spoke to him. When he finished, the man mounted his horse and proceeded toward the guards' shack at the end of the tree-lined pathway.

Some men snickered, but the others had seen the young woman ride bareback and thought the outcome would surprise the boss.

"Well, let's get to it." Miliya reined her white stallion Cloud next to Lightning whose owner with a huge smile on his handsome face sat erect, atop his back. .

It seemed, in seconds, they were passing the house with Nakai in the lead and Miliya close behind. She waved at an astonished Mama Louise, who, after hearing a gunshot, ran out on the porch, flailing a black skillet, her eyes wild. Imagine her surprise when the Nakai and his lady soared by on their stallions, Miliya's honey blonde hair flying behind in wild abandonment.

As they approached the two guards, Stone and Abraham, slight smiles covered their solemn faces as Nakai and Miliya whizzed by. She was quite a woman, Stone thought. Not too many ladies could boast they ride bareback as good as any man. Without a doubt, the boss had a special lady.

The pair was nearing the overhead Kensington Estate wrought iron sign. Nakai was still in the lead, Miliya a yard behind.

Nakai looked behind him at the beautiful woman. The sun's rays illuminated her honey-blonde hair creating, a golden halo around her head. She wore a determined look on her face. He had to win! He remembered when Zelia had the ladies from the Guild over. They chit chatted for over an hour about nothing, and he never did see much sewing get done. His lips curled. That will not be his worry today since he would win. Glad she can cook, he thought.

But it doesn't matter; she'd have a week to perfect her culinary skills. On their way back, the two guards watched their boss whiz by, pursued by his strong-willed woman!

Miliya smiled. It's not over yet, Mr. Kensington! She pressed her feet into the sides of Cloud, spurring the stallion forward. Trees whooshed by in a blur as they neared the house. Louise stood on the porch hollering Miliya's name as they passed by. Curiosity beckoned the housekeeper to rush to the corrals to see who won.

His brother was the first to speak. "Well, I can take care of the ranch, since you'll be in town most of the week."

Several men did their best not to laugh, but a sneer escaped the lips of one man. A hush swept over the men, but all eyes were on their boss who held out his hand to Miliya and said, "Well done."

The compliment from a skilled horseman of his well-known reputation gave her immense pleasure. His hand engulfed hers with a firm shake.

Seeing that the boss accepted his loss with a sporting attitude, the men congratulated him for one heck of a race. Their boss was always fair, but since Miss Miliya entered his life, he had become more tolerant of certain situations. Where before, he would act like an angry mountain lion; now he purred like a kitten. Not to say he was a pushover. Harm Miss Miliya or his family and hell couldn't hide you.

A minute later the estate matriarch, huffing and puffing, joined them.

"Lord, child, you rode like the devil was on your back! Never saw such riding from a woman." Louise turned her gaze to the man standing next to her.

"I credit my ability to the survival techniques, including riding bareback, taught to me by Grandpa Peter and the family friend, Mary Fields, known as the legendary Stagecoach Mary. She carried and used a gun with the proficiency of an experienced gunslinger.

"Grandpa Peter asked her to teach me how to shoot."

"You shoot too?" Nakai cocked a brow in surprise.

"Don't worry, love. I won't shoot you." She pecked him on the cheek. "Unless you make me mad."

Louise steered the conversation back to the race. "As the loser, what was your reward?"

"I get to accompany her to the Ladies' Guild starting today and if she desires for this entire week." He twisted his mouth into a wry grin.

"Aww, that's not so bad." Louise smiled back.

"Yes, it is! I get to watch them ladies caterwaul for an hour. Can't even wait in the buggy. There are a million things I could do here." Nakai sounded like a petulant child.

Glaring at him, Miliya said, "I can drop the sewing, but the dinner at Nicoles stays."

Ashamed, Nakai felt like a spoilsport. A wager is a wager. He thought he would be the winner, but she proved him wrong. Didn't he tell her to prove she was the best?

"No, you're right. You won fair and square. I'll honor both of your conditions."

"Not to interfere with your duties as head of Kensington Estates, Friday night at Nicoles is all I want," she replied.

"As agreed, for the next month, every Friday we would dine at Nicoles." The facial expression of the woman he treasured lit up like lights on a Christmas tree. She grabbed him about his neck and kissed his cheek.

"Thank you, thank you, thank you!" Miliya repeated. The men whistled, laughing at the obvious embarrassment of their boss.

"Gee, Miliya," Royce began, "I looked forward to seeing big brother check his stitches on a dress and holding it up for the ladies' approval."

Without a word, Nakai picked up the lariat Royce held earlier, threw the rope around his brother's body, enclosing his arms. Securing the cord around the bottom corral fence forced his struggling younger brother to fall to the ground on his bottom.

"Ah, come on. This rope is tight. I will lose circulation in my arms!"

"Men," Nakai said, "the excitement is over now. Thanks for the support. Please return to your duties."

The assembly of men dispersed, talking amongst themselves and looking back at the ranch manager trussed up like a turkey, sitting in the dirt and yelling for his brother to free him.

"Let's go, ladies," Nakai held out his arms. "It's lunchtime, and I've worked up an appetite." Each woman tucked her arm under his, and then they walked towards the house in amiable conversation.

"Hey, loosen me, has everyone lost their minds?" Royce hollered.

Eight o'clock, that night, Nakai ordered his release.

CHAPTER 19

Miliya and Nakai stood among Mt. Bethel members and a small group of people at a freshly dug grave, their faces solemn as Pastor Owens spoke.

"Sister Christine accepted Christ a year ago and has been a faithful member ever since. She had no family, except a female cousin, but her whereabouts are not known. Today we commit her body to the ground, but her spirit belongs to God."

After he prayed, people greeted each other before they moved to the church for repast. A young woman, dressed in a black dress and a shawl, wept by a tree. She wiped her eyes and followed the path back towards town.

"I wonder if that lady is Christine's cousin," Miliya said, nudging Nakai. He turned and saw a woman crying, shoulders slumped, her heart wrenching sobs echoed around the quiet graveyard.

"It could be," Nakai answered. "Let's give her a ride home."

Nakai aimed the carriage in the woman's direction. Seconds later, he navigated the horses alongside the woman. Wary, she stopped and looked askance at the couple.

"Hello, was Christine your cousin?" Miliya asked.

"Yes," she asserted. Fresh tears escaped down her tear-stained face.

"I'm sorry for your loss. My name is Miliya Davis, and this gentleman is Nakai Kensington." The woman's head twisted around. Her eyes flashed hate.

"Nakai Kensington! You are the reason she's dead!" Her accusation startled them.

"Why would you say that?" Frowning, Miliya retorted.

"Christine loved you, mister, forever it seemed, but you never gave her the time of day! That's why she helped him to get back at you!"

Nakai and Miliya traded looks. Him? Could it be the man trying to kill her?

He dismounted from the carriage and walked over to the woman. She stepped back.

"What is your name?" Nakai asked. Thinking he'd seen her before somewhere.

"Joyce."

"Joyce, I am sorry for your loss. I didn't know Christine, but she appeared to be an amiable person."

"How would you know? You said you didn't know her." The woman sneered.

"Nakai, let me explain since I was there," Miliya said. In response he stepped to the side.

"Joyce, Christine, and I were standing together at the basket bidding. She told me about her attraction to Nakai. She also asked God's forgiveness and said, 'I can't let him do this!'" Miliya paused,

180

"Christine saved my life. She knew this man meant to shoot me, and she impeded the bullet. An unselfish act by a person who realized vengeance belonged to God."

"Joyce, do you know the man she was talking about?" Nakai asked. Something flickered in her eyes, then disappeared.

She shrugged her slight shoulders. "She only talked about you."

"If you don't want to tell me what you know, tell Sheriff Raven," Nakai said. "This person had tried to kill Miliya twice, and he had taken the life of your cousin."

Joyce cocked her head at the handsome man.

"You sure you can't think of anything?" Nakai repeated.

"I know nothing." She wiped her eyes with the handkerchief.

"Can we give you a lift into town?"

"No, thank you, I feel like walking." A slight smile curved her lips.

"Once again, we are sorry for your loss."

The young woman nodded and headed down the well-beaten path to Pinesdale.

"Did you get the feeling she knew more than what she admitted?" Miliya frowned.

Focusing his attention on the road. Nakai agreed. "I do. I've seen her before."

"Where?" Miliya asked.

181

His answer would reveal the one time in his life he wasn't proud of his actions. Would she judge me on that one time?

"After Zelia left town, I felt discouraged. She had rejected my selfless love. One day, while in town, I indulged my sorrows at the saloon.."

"Oh, Nakai," Miliya whispered.

He grimaced. "While I was making a complete idiot of myself, one of the fancy ladies accosted me. By then, I was entering the realm of intoxication. Before I embarrassed myself and the Kensington name, I went home. But I remember Joyce because she helped me to my horse."

"That was considerate of her, "Miliya murmured.

Moments passed before anyone said a word.

His eyes touched her face. "Have your thoughts changed about me now that I shared this with you?"

Miliya reached over and kissed his cheek. "Not at all. As humans, we tend to look for ways to rid ourselves of the hurt and disappointments in our lives instead of remembering the Lord was near and ready to embrace us with His peace."

The words I love you almost slipped from his lips. Nakai wanted her love and her hand in marriage. Lord, tell me when it's time to confess my love to her.

"Repentant prayers back then were as much a part of my life as breathing, even today," he admitted.

"You're not alone. Me too." The earnestness in her voice made him turn towards her.

"You? Repentant about what?" Nakai was interested; he couldn't conceive what problem she had. To him, she was perfect.

182

Miliya nibbled on her bottom lip, a habit she had when nervous. The lump in her throat threatened to choke her words.

"Maybe another time?" He saw her hesitation.

"Now is fine. If we are to have a meaningful relationship, we need to share our strengths and weaknesses." Gazing at the countryside, she began her story.

"I questioned the way God created me. When I was around seven years old, I was taller than most of the kids in school. They would call me a giant breed, cracker girl, and a tall, blue-eyed witch." She lifted her eyes from her lap to his dark gaze.

"They were just ignorant!" His voice rumbled with anger.

"I had low self-esteem most of my school days until I matured, and then the boys called me a blue-eyed beauty, with hair the color of butterscotch."

He let out a harsh breath.

"Girls snubbed me because the boys found me pretty and different, their words, so I didn't have girlfriends except for Serenity, who lived with her family down the road from my grandparent's farm. She never judged me but treated me more like a sister."

"I suppose your grandparents were very concerned about you."

"That's why Grandpa Peter taught me how to survive in the woods, how to ride and shoot. In case anyone attempted to harm me, I could protect myself."

Nakai glanced over at Miliya. She proved her competence as a horsewoman, and she can shoot a gun. His lady was self-sufficient.

"Do you have those insecurities now?" He nodded to Stone as they reached the guard shack. Miliya fiddled with the purse in her lap. Her head bent.

"Miliya?" Nakai said, "Look at me."

When she lifted her head, her blue eyes shimmered with tears. "Yes." Her voice trembled.

Nakai pulled back on the reins, rendering the horses to a complete stop. He placed the reins on the seat. He moved over and with his thumbs gently wiped the tears from her eyes.

"Look at me," he demanded; his voice terse. Startled, she faced him.

He met her gaze. "Do you feel insecure around me?"

"Yes." The semi-smile on her face faltered.

"Why?" he breathed. Disbelief manipulated his brown face.

"It goes back to my childhood days as I said. My height, for instance. I'm taller than the average woman. When Zelia came by the other day, I noticed she was of medium height, she'd have to stand on a chair to kiss you. This was the woman you loved; a short woman."

"Stop!" Nakai yelled, closing his eyes. He drew in a long breath and breathed out. When he did face her, she sat with her arms folded around herself. A look of bewilderment covered her features.

Long fingers gently cupped her chin and pinned her with his deep brown eyes.

"As long as you are in my presence, never compare or downgrade yourself. You are the woman in my heart, a balm to my soul, and no other woman from the past or the future will ever take your place. Not only are you attractive, but also a humble, loving person, and I will not tolerate you thinking otherwise. God meant you to be tall

184

and beautiful and a gift to me; accept the audacious woman you are." He gave a lopsided grin. "Okay?" Tears ran down her cheeks. She bobbed her head.

"Is everything all right, Nakai?" Stone called out as he approached the buggy on horseback. His eyes trained on Miliya's tear-stained face.

"Yes. Thanks for your concern Stone."

The guard glanced over at the tremulous smile on the young woman. He nodded and rode back to where Abraham stood watching.

Nakai shook his head. Every man on the estates was fond of his woman. If they stayed in their place, they could be her champion all day long. However, Royce may have a different view on it, since he claimed that position from the day, she entered their lives.

"Are you hungry?" Nakai asked, picking up the reins, he gave one whack and directed the horses towards the homestead.

"I am," she admitted. "I thought you could mention to Raven to keep an eye on Joyce, just in case she's not telling us the truth, and this person tried to contact her. It was just a thought."

"Sounds like a good idea. I'll speak with Raven when I see him, later, tonight."

Reaching the house, he vaulted from the carriage, tied the reins to the hitching post, and went around to where Miliya sat. Taking her hand as she stepped down.

"Nakai?" He lowered his eyes at her with raised brows. She hugged his waist. His arms embraced her. They stood there for a few moments before she released him. "Thank you."

"I'm always here for you; remember that." He tweaked her nose.

"Let's go in and see what culinary specialty Louise has prepared for us today."

Holding hands, they walked into the house.

Joyce headed down the well-beaten path to Pinesdale deep in thought. Two years ago, the striking Nakai Kensington happened in the saloon, quiet, unapproachable, and despondent. He became intoxicated, and she had tried to seduce him, but she felt pity for the rancher and had helped him onto his horse before he made a spectacle of himself. She understood the fascination Christine had for him. He was a gentleman. If she revealed what she knew, could he or Sheriff Raven protect her from that insane killer?

Last week, Jake had stolen out into the night, to hide out in the woods. He didn't reveal his secret, and she didn't ask. The less she knew, the better for her. Yet, he killed Christine; shouldn't he pay for his crime?

"She what?" Jake banged his fist on the table. "Are you sure?"

The man cleared his throat. "I saw your girlfriend talking to Nakai Kensington and his woman at her cousin's funeral today. Do you remember her cousin? The woman you shot and killed by mistake!" His whiny voice sounded shriller than usual.

Jake moved in one swift movement and grabbed the man by his slim neck and shoved him against the wall with both hands. His dark eyes hardened with hate, and his nostrils flared.

"You little wannabe, talk like that again, and you might get shot and killed by mistake!" His hands tightened, then slowly released the hold on his throat.

Adjusting his bowtie, he said in a raspy voice, "You don't have to get physical. What are you going to do about this new development?"

Jake glared at his employer. When he finished this job, he would cut out his sarcastic tongue. "You bring the woman here. I'll tell her what to say to Kensington."

"When and where would they meet?"

"I haven't decided. One thing at a time. Bring her here tomorrow." Jake sat down at the table, reached for the bottle of liquor, unscrewed the top, and guzzled half of the brown liquid in the bottle

"Tomorrow," the employer said. As he walked out the door. His patience for the vile man had run out. This week he would take what the owner of Kensington Estate loved the most in life; Miliya.

CHAPTER 20

This is the day the Lord has made; I will rejoice and be glad in it. I'm expecting something good to happen to me and through me today, Lord. Direct my steps onto the path you want me to go. Thank you for your favor that surrounds me like a shield and thank you for our Lord Jesus Christ, the greatest gift to man. Amen.

Miliya rose from her knees, donned the white cotton robe, and walked over to the bedroom window. Royce, Nakai, and a few of the men conversed at the corral fence. Respectful of the brother's privacy, the men dispersed when Raven joined them.

At dinner last night, Nakai told Raven he believed Joyce knew more than what she revealed. She wondered if she gave him any information. A few minutes later, Raven galloped away. As he passed by the house, he gazed at her window; waved, and rode on.

There was a knock at the door. A warm scent of woods, patchouli and leather arrested her nose when she opened the door. The man of her dreams stood holding a cup of coffee in his right hand, and a black ledger underneath his left arm.

"Good morning, beautiful." His dark gaze examined her face.

"Good morning to you, sir." Her smile brightened the room. "Coffee for me?"

"Sorry, my dear, this cup is mine. Mama Louise sent me to ask you, are you waiting for lunchtime, to come to breakfast?" He shrugged his broad shoulders.

"Were those her words?" A wary smile surfaced on her face.

"Yes, ma'am! I'm an innocent bystander heading to my office. There is a pile of paperwork that needs my attention."

"All right. I'll see you for lunch."

 "Don't forget to eat light. Nicoles tonight." Humming, he moved down the hallway, two doors down to his office.

Her heart pounded like a bass drum; it was beating so hard. Miliya couldn't wait for the day she could express her love for him. Rejection had been her constant companion in her youth. Through the years, she had learned to harbor her emotions. The healing process began after she had revealed her insecurities to Nakai, the one man she didn't want to know about her vulnerabilities. There was anger and hurt as he had gazed at her; but after his motivational words, acceptance and love shone within the depths of his deep brown eyes. God loved her and she felt Nakai did too. Fear was rejection's friend, and she casted the two into the sea of forgetfulness. Through the power of Jesus, she forgave herself, so she could be free to love more. God didn't bring them together for her to allow lack of self-confidence to block their divine connection. Her trust is in God's timing. She sat down at the dresser and began brushing her hair. Tonight, her reward for winning the race, Nakai was treating her to dinner at Nicoles. She planned to wear one of the Parisian

originals from Miriams Dress Shop purchased weeks ago. Miliya dressed, and went downstairs for breakfast.

Nakai leaned back in the leather chair, thanking God he could restrain himself when around the tall, enthralling woman down the hall. He longed for a long term relationship with Miliya; kissing included. He snickered. The picture of how she'd brought Ed Masters to his knees that day on the church grounds nullified any further thoughts on the kissing matter!

Nakai informed Stone as they stood on the porch. "Tonight, Miliya and I are going out to dine at Nicoles, you can have the night off."

"Yes sir." The Creole nodded. He gazed at his boss. "Your lady's riding skills surpass most men." Miliya had raced Stone to the corral from one of her jaunts around the property. The guard was glad no one was around to see her beat him by at least a foot.

"Best I've ever seen; man or woman," Stone admitted.

"She beat you too?" Nakai asked, grinning at the lopsided smile on the Creole's face.

"Me too, course I couldn't let her know, a man's ego and all understand?"

His boss grinned. "Understood."

Stone appreciated the night off, but until they apprehended this maniac, concern for Miliya's safety was foremost on his mind. Being a man who abstained from all liquor, he saw no problem riding to town and partaking of a fine meal at Sarah's, in particular, her peach cobbler. While there, he would visit the sheriff's office and check if Raven had any new leads. He heard the clatter of the carriage pass by the shack. The guard wanted to be far enough behind them so they wouldn't sense his presence, but close enough in case they needed help. Before mounting his horse he waited a few minutes to allow distance between him and his boss.

Spewing cuss words, Jake paced back and forth in the cabin. Where is the sniveling wannabe? Earlier, he had sneaked into town, brought the strumpet to the hideout, and threatened her life if she ratted on him. He had requested an extra one hundred dollars from the weasel. Those few dollars the wannabe paid him weren't worth the crap he was going through! The Kensingtons have made this killing complicated. One thousand-dollar reward? It tempted him to surrender for that amount of money! He will leave this town once the whiner gives him the money.

A creaking sound of the door alerted Jake. He jerked his head in time to see the barrel of a gun thrust through the slight opening. Jake went for his gun on the table, and his last rational thought was that two-timing weasel!

Nakai escorted Miliya into the crowded restaurant. He wanted this evening to be memorable for his lady, and she deserved the royal treatment. The waitress greeted them with a brilliant smile.

"This way, Mr. Kensington."

They followed the young woman to a secluded table near the rear of the room. Wildflowers, Miliya's favorite, adorned the center of the table

Nakai pulled out her chair, then seated himself.

"What will you have to drink, madam?" The waitress asked, handing each one a menu.

"Lemonade," Miliya said.

"And your order, sir?"

"Apple cider."

"I shall return with your drinks," she proceeded to the kitchen.

Miliya glanced around at the opulent room. This evening was the second time she had visited the establishment. Each time she noticed something different such as the painting on the wall behind Nakai, of The Eiffel Tower lit up at night, spectacular. One day, she would not hesitate to visit France to see the iron structure adorning the rooftops of Paris and the other breathtaking sites of the city and countryside.

"A penny for your thoughts," Nakai said.

She blushed. "I was admiring the painting of the Eiffel Tower on the wall behind you."

He twisted around, staring at the painting. His mouth pouted.

"Oh, I thought those beautiful eyes were admiring me, not a French painting!" He clutched his chest. "My heart is wounded."

"You are a work of art."

Oh goodness! Did she sound like a lovesick schoolgirl?

For a moment, he appeared stunned but allowed himself an extra second to regard the woman facing him. Did he hear love in her words? Lord, I know she cares for me, but is she in love with me? Is she ready to tell me? Or am I hearing what I want to hear because I love her?

"Thank you for the compliment." His eyes held hers.

"Welcome." She blushed.

The waitress returned with their drinks and took their orders. Once again, she moved to the kitchen.

"Are you Mr. Kensington?" An elderly gentleman asked, standing at their table. His sudden presence surprised the couple.

"Yes," he answered, his brow lifted. "Who wants to know?" Cautious, Nakai stood, his six feet six inches towered over the man.

Fear crossed his face. The man gave a quick response to the overwhelming figure standing in front of him.

"The young woman over by the front door asked me to tell you to meet her outside for a minute

Nakai's eyes traveled to the restaurant entrance. No woman stood there; she must be outside. Who could it be?

"Miliya, I don't know who this is, but I hope it's Joyce, with some information to catch the shooter."

"Be careful, Nakai." He leaned down and kissed her cheek.

"I'll be right back."

Miliya watched him walk through the door. Anxiety washed over her blue eyes. Chills broke out on her arms, and she threw her wrap around her shoulders. Call it a prompting, or woman's intuition, but she had an ominous feeling about this meeting.

"Hello, Miliya."

Surprise ignited in her eyes at Clyde Miller, standing at the table, holding his hat in his hand.

"Hello, Clyde. I didn't see you."

"I saw you and Kensington come in." His voice was chilled, reproachful.

"He had to step out for a minute."

"I know." He raised his hat and revealed a gun pointing at her.

"Now, you will stand up and walk in front of me out the back door."

Her eyes darted to the front door, then to the back exit. Clyde sniggered. "Do anything other than what I request, and you and your Injun boyfriend will die. His usual friendly eyes had transformed into that of a malicious person glaring down at her.

"What's it going to be, Miliya?"

"Nakai will be back in a minute."

He let out a mocking laugh, "He's busy! Let's go! Else, I'll walk out there and shoot him d-e-a-d dead!"

Miliya wondered how he knew what Nakai was doing. Did he send a woman to be a diversion, so he could sneak in here and kidnap her? Mr. Miller wasn't the mild-mannered man he portrayed in public. She succumbed to his request to prevent unnecessary loss of life; this was not the time to thwart him.

Her legs trembled as she rose from the chair and moved toward the door, shadowed by Clyde.

"Joyce, what information do you have for me?"

Nakai watched the woman pull the black wrap tighter around the blue velvet dress. Her black hair was pulled back in a braid, and her brown eyes were huge in her brown face.

"I know where the shooter is." She cleared her throat.

"And where is that?"

"I can show you better than I can tell you."

"That's good news! Have you told Sheriff Raven?"

Her eyes lowered to the ground. "No. I thought you might want to get a head start; I mean, since it's your woman, he's aiming to kill!"

"That may be true, but Raven is the law in these parts, and this man is a wanted killer. He must uphold the law and apprehend him."

She nibbled her bottom lip. "I'll talk to him."

"Miliya is inside. I will tell her what has transpired and when we go to the sheriff's office, she will be left there in the protection of one of the deputies until we return."

The woman glanced around, her eyes darting back and forth, biting down on her lip. His senses switched on full alert. Something's wrong!

"The truth, Joyce! Now!" His voice commanded. Nakai Kensington stood with arms crossed.

"I have told the—"

The impatient man held his hand up, halting her words. "I consider myself a man that believes and accepts Jesus Christ and his teachings. I am a peaceful man, but when my loved ones are in danger, I become territorial. I will do pretty much what I need to do to ensure their safety. What can I say? I'm a work in progress. Do I make myself clear?" He took a slight step forward.

Trembling, Joyce swallowed, wishing she never had any dealings with Jake.

"I met him, the killer, in the saloon three weeks ago. Some man hired him to kill your lady. When he found out Christine had a vendetta against you, he used her to get any information about Miliya."

"Who is the man who hired this killer?"

"Jake. The killer's name is Jake. I don't know who hired him.

They met in secret; he didn't say where and I asked no questions."

"Why say something now?"

Joyce casts her troubled look downwards and took a trembling breath.

"Yesterday, Jake took me to his hideout where he threatened me; that if I said anything, I'd receive what my cousin did." Her doleful eyes implored his forgiveness. Which he ignored.

"How did he know we would be here today?"

"Was this his plan for you to distract me so he could kidnap Miliya?" Nakai rebuked.

"Not him: his boss!" Tears flooded her eyes. "I realized I have sent the innocent young woman to her death!"

The oldest Kensington brother flung open the restaurant door and hurried over to the table where he had left Miliya. Her wrap laid on the table along with her purse.

"He took her!" He raked his fingers through his hair.

"Oh, there you are." The relieved voice of the waitress triggered Nakai's attention; his brows lifted. The woman explained.

"I saw you leave and then a few minutes later your lady left with Mr. Miller. I wondered…"

"Clyde Miller?" Nakai asked, chopping off her words. His bass voice rumbled in disbelief.

"Yes. Every Saturday he dines by himself, but tonight I saw him talking with a woman." She glanced around his imposing body. "That woman."

Without turning around, he knew she was pointing to Joyce. She appeared troubled and took a trembling breath.

"When did they leave?"

"About five minutes after you left, by the back door in which I thought was a little odd." She frowned.

Nakai reached into his jacket pocket, retrieved his leather pouch, and passed the waitress a few coins.

"For the bill."

"Thank you, sir, but…" She broke off. The awe-inspiring man had turned away from her to grasp the wrap lying atop the table.

"What now?" Joyce asked, wringing her hands.

"We're going to Raven's office and bring him up to date with the latest information. Then you will take us to where Miller took Miliya."

Joyce shuddered at the low, deadly voice. Unflinching eyes bore into her. She cleared her throat. "I'll do my best. Yesterday was the first time I've ever been there. But I do know it's a straight way from town."

"Let's go. We've already wasted too much time."

The man and woman left the restaurant en-route to the Sheriff's office.

Stone had followed his boss and his lady to Nicoles restaurant and slipped into Sarah's, across the street from Nicoles, his intent to monitor the couple. The waitress had just given him a menu when his boss walked through the front door. A saloon girl approached Nakai and engaged him in conversation. Within seconds his boss appeared agitated before he rushed back into the building, followed

by the woman. An ominous feeling crept over him. Something was wrong! At that moment, he knew someone had taken Miliya!

CHAPTER 21

"Clyde Miller?" Raven said, shocked.

"Who's Clyde Miller?" Stone asked, striding through the office door.

Nakai slid questioning, eyes at his employee. "What are you doing here? I gave you a day off."

Stone had the chagrin to smile. "I was dining across the street from Nicoles at Sarah's when to my surprise, I saw you and a woman leave the restaurant... without Miss Miliya."

"Thanks for having our backs."

"Who's this Miller guy?"

"A Pinesdale banker who hired a hitman to kill Miliya." Nakai answered. with clenched fists.

"Do you know where he took her?" Stone asked.

The brothers gazed over at the woman sitting in the chair at Raven's desk. Stone's light brown eyes assessed the trembling young woman. Joyce regarded the guard with a look of curiosity. A light flickered in the depths of his eyes. she withered under the cold; scrutiny of the striking man dressed in black.

Nakai leaned against the desk, watching Stone and the incensed attitude he was displaying. No one felt more outrage than he did, but this young woman was a victim as well, something he needed to remind himself.

"Well, why are we still here?" Stone wanted to know.

"We were just about to go when you walked in." The woman and three men exited the office mounted their horses and galloped hard into the woods.

Jake's Hideout

"Stop tugging on the ropes! I'd have to tighten them more; then you'd have a permanent bruise on your wrists; wouldn't want to mar that pale skin," Clyde sneered. He placed his gun on the table.

"Why are you doing this?" Miliya asked, twisting her hands, trying to loosen the tight knot.

"You can ask that?" He glared at her with maniacal eyes.

"What have I done to provoke such hate?"

His deranged laugh reverberated in the abandoned shack.

"Let me refresh your memory! Remember, at your get-together when you thought it cute to play a joke on the banker, pretending your 'savage' was behind me? Your insensitivity caused me to make a slight mishap on the floor in full view of everyone. I've yet to live it down!" His eyes were huge and wild on his face.

Miliya heard the pain in his voice and closed her eyes, recalling that night. Several men had stepped on her toes, Clyde being the worse, and she wanted release from the painful torment. Yes, she took advantage of his fear of Nakai to get relief. It was wrong, and the result of that decision has placed her in a life-threatening position.

Lord, I'm sorry, forgive my insensitivity towards Clyde; I didn't intend to hurt him. Please remove all selfishness harboring in my heart and fill me with compassion and humility to love others when I'm self-absorbed.

Her eyes glittered with tears as she met the hurt and ire in his eyes.

"I'm sorry, Clyde. Forgive me for any pain my inconsideration has caused you."

His frenzied laughter mocked her sincerity. "I'm sorry, Clyde," he mimicked, pacing in front of her. "Momentary pain in your feet doesn't compare to a lifetime of cruelty."

"How did you know we would be at Nicoles tonight?"

"By accident." He grinned at her confused look. "Yesterday, when I spoke to the waitress to confirm my standing reservation for tonight, I saw Nakai's reservation on the list for tonight. I knew you would be with him, so I hatched my plan."

"Clyde, you aren't a killer."

"Oh, but I am."

Milya froze. "Who?"

"My hitman. I buried him in the back." The banker waited for her to absorb his words. "The vile man was too bossy, so I had to get rid of him, and now I will take care of you."

"What do you want from me?"

Clyde crouched down until he was at eye level. He reached out and grabbed a handful of hair and yanked her to him.

"You, as my wife."

"Where will Nakai be?"

"Dead." His voice was cold, heartless.

Miliya raised her brows, her jaw dropped. "Clyde, every Sunday Pastor Dave spoke to the congregation that God loves us unconditionally. I know you heard him. You sat behind me every Sunday sneezing and sniffing."

" I have sinus issues," he said.

Miliya continued. "The bible says, 'do not murder. What you reap you will sow.' Our Lord loves us no matter what we've done. However, we will suffer the consequences of our sins."

Indignation shown on Clyde's face. "Even, if he was an overbearing, rude, cocky person?"

"The bible says, 'do not murder. What you reap you will sow.'"

She glanced at him in unbelief. "That is no reason to kill someone!"

"He bullied me one time too many," he said coolly.

Exasperated, she looked at him. "You must not avenge yourself, but when someone hurts you, because God said, 'Vengeance is mine. I will repay.' Do you love Jesus?"

He directed his woeful eyes at Miliya, and said quietly, "Yes."

"He loves you too, more than you'll ever know. Although you stepped into the realm of darkness, the Lord, is the Light of the world and awaits you with open arms. How can you refuse His love and mercy?"

He ran his hand over his face. "Pastor Dave said we must repent of our sins."

"Clyde, then confess your sin, admit your wrongdoing, and forgive. Forgiveness is a choice. Forgive those who have hurt you, even if

they knew of their actions. If not, God will not forgive your iniquities. Some people are unaware that their actions have caused others pain."

"Like you?"

"Believe me, I didn't think you would be affected as much as you were. I would never have put you through this. Forgive yourself. Receive God's forgiveness, so that His grace can flow through your life. Then, forgive God. Decisions we make come back to haunt us, but don't blame God. Remember, think on His word and leave the rest up to Him."

A loud sob reverberated through the cabin as Clyde fell to his knees. Remorseful, he held his head in his hands and began to sob.

"Forgive me, God! I repent of my sins!" He raised his head to look at Miliya. "I forgive you for what you did. Can you forgive me? Jealousy and pride caused my spiteful behavior." Tears ran down his face.

Overwhelmed with emotion, Miliya said, "Yes. I forgive you."

Outside, help had arrived!

Raven, Stone, Nakai, and Joyce hid behind a clump of dense bushes a few feet away from the run-down shack.

"Stone, cover the back. We," Raven glanced at Nakai, "have the front."

Nodding, with the stealth and grace of a panther, Stone disappeared around the building.

Nakai glanced across at the young woman holding her wrap snug about her chest.

"Stay hidden."

Swallowing, she nodded and crouched closer behind the foliage.

"Do nothing rash," his brother ordered, looking over his shoulder at Nakai.

"If he hurts Miliya, I will be the last thing he sees." His jaw tightened.

Raven dipped his head. "We love her too. She's the sister we never had. Falcon and Royce will be mad they weren't here to help capture Clyde. We will rescue her, unharmed." He signaled to advance towards the shack.

Silent steps carried them into the room unnoticed. Disbelief colored their vision at the sight of the banker sobbing and holding his head in front of Miliya. Why is it that men who try to harm this woman end up pleading for her forgiveness? No one could tell Nakai she wasn't an angel; his angel.

Raven dashed over to the distraught man and handcuffed him with no resistance. He pulled Clyde to his feet and turned him to face the man he had hated with all his heart. Nakai retrieved the knife from the sheath strapped about his leg and cut the ropes binding Miliya's wrists. Rubbing her reddened wrists, he kissed each one and pulled her into his arms. He would have held her forever, but he remembered the other two men. His intense eyes penetrated the downtrodden stare of the younger man. He moved toward him.

"Nakai?" Miliya placed her hand on his sleeve. He acknowledged

her worried look with a nod.

"Clyde, if anyone would have asked me, what would you do to the person responsible for the pain and madness of the past month? I'd say one word. Death!"

The sable skin man flinched, eyes downcast, averting his vengeful gaze.

"I won't lie," Nakai confessed. "My hands are clenching by my sides because I want to strangle you, but I overheard your conversation with Miliya, and I want to say I forgive you. Until I met this lady, my anger and bitterness controlled my life." He peered at Miliya leaning against him, and continued.

"This woman helped me to understand unforgiveness delays the blessings of our heavenly Father; that whenever you forgive others, His favor increases in your life. God is not a respecter of persons If he did it for me, he'll do it for you."

The banker nodded, too emotional to speak. At that moment, the back door opened and Stone emerged through the portal. He acknowledged everyone with a slight nod of his head.

"There's a fresh grave out back."

"That's the hitman," Raven answered.

Stone walked over to where Miliya stood next to Nakai, his arm draped around her shoulder and her head rested on his chest.

"Miss Miliya, are you all right?" The deep timbre of his voice reflected concern.

"Fine… now," she said gazing up into Nakai's loving eyes.

"I thank you all for coming to my rescue. How did you find me?"

"Joyce. She was the woman outside the restaurant," Nakai replied.

"Speaking of which, she's outside hiding," Raven said. "Nothing else to do here. Miliya, I'll get your statement tomorrow. Go home; you've had enough excitement for today."

Nakai, Miliya, and Joyce took the carriage Clyde had driven earlier. Lightning and Joyce's horse were tied to the back of the carriage, and then the threesome rode back to town in silence.

That night, the Kensington brothers sat in the parlor, discussing the day's events.

"Well, big brother, I'm glad Miliya is all right, and I didn't have to hurt anyone."

Looking at his youngest brother. Nakai mused, "No one is gladder than me. We didn't have time to tell you, Falcon and Dakota of our plans."

"Thank God you were able to rescue her and arrest Clyde without any harm done to either. I still can't believe his involvement in the scheme to have Miliya murdered."

"He wanted her, she rejected him, and he hated me because, in his mind, I was in his way to have her. By murdering her, he would kill two birds with one stone. One, he would hurt me, and two, he would avenge her rejection of him. Jealousy, anger, and vengeance triggered his temporary madness," Nakai concluded.

"What's hard to understand is you forgave him, Nakai! As much as you care for Miliya, you forgave the one man who meant her harm." Royce shook his head in disbelief.

Four pairs of eyes gravitated towards the oldest Kensington brother.

"I can because I choose to. God has sent me one of his angels to walk with me through life and beyond, and I'm thankful to be blessed by Him. He tells us to forgive our enemies as He has forgiven us through Christ Jesus. God will make it right," Nakai said.

The silence in the room was audible. Each brother was in awe and inspired by the sincere words spoken by their brother.

Royce studied Nakai with wide greenish-brown eyes. "Amen," he said in a hoarse voice.

"Does Miliya know the depth of your love?" Dakota asked Nakai.

"I don't know. She knows my admiration towards her goes beyond friendship."

"Why haven't you told her how you feel?" Falcon searched his face.

"We've known each other for a month now, although longer for me through my dreams, but I don't know if she is ready to commit. Until she tells me otherwise, I won't pressure her." Falcon agreed.

Bethel Church

Sunday morning

"Before they read the announcements, I would like to talk about a matter that affects us, and two of our members. Talk around the community is they arrested Brother Clyde Miller for kidnapping and murder." Pastor Evans gazed around the whispering congregation before continuing. "Our Father says in Luke 6: 37, "Judge not, and ye shall not be judged: condemn not and ye shall not be condemned: forgive, and ye shall be forgiven. Let us not get caught up in gossip and be judgmental but pray that God works His perfect will in this young man's life." He gauged the congregation.

"As a victim of this wickedness, we must give God the glory and praise for assigning his angels to protect Sister Miliya during this time."

The older man smiled, looking over toward the Kensington pew. "Let us pray." Heads bowed as the somber-faced Pastor led his flock in prayer.

Nakai peered at the woman sitting next to him, dabbing her eyes with a handkerchief. Honey brown hair flowed around her shoulders, spilling down the front of her emerald green jacket. Lord, I am thankful that You kept Miliya safe and unharmed throughout this entire ordeal, and I praise you for your love and mercy. In your time, Lord, this woman will become my wife. Satisfied with that thought, he bowed his head in prayer.

Two weeks later, Raven told his brothers and Miliya that Clyde Miller pleaded guilty and was sentenced to ten years in the Old Montana Prison in Butte, Montana.

Nakai shut the ledger and shoved it across his desk. His mind wasn't on the figures on those pages, but Miliya Davis. Miliya had moved her belongings back to the guest house days after Raven jailed Clyde. He missed her presence. Monday, his friend David Merrick, owner of a horse ranch in Denver, and two other prospective buyers arrived in town to look at the Kensington stock of trained horses. It so happened that an Arabian, two Thoroughbreds, and a Mustang were for sale. Four examples of exquisite horseflesh. With meetings and paperwork, Nakai had little time left but to eat; and when he did, he was in town transacting business with his friend and the other gentlemen at the Pinesdale Hotel. He missed her. When he has completed negotiations, he will give her a big bear hug and say, 'I love you.' Lord, it's time.

He rose from his seat and strolled over to the window, watching the guest house with longing. Wait a minute! Who was that man at the door? Nothing had changed. All safety precautions were still the same. All male visitors, other than relatives, must meet Miliya at the estate. Recognition dawned on his face. Bash! Why was he at Miliya's door?

Nakai slammed his fist down onto the desk when his friend dipped his head, then closed the door. Did he kiss her? Heat began rising like the yeast in Mama Louise's rolls. His chest rose and fell with rapid breaths. Calm down, he chided himself. Cast down any negative thoughts. There is a logical explanation and he's not waiting for another second to find out! Determined, the Master of Kensington Estates strode out the room.

"Kayja!" Bash bent his head and kissed the exuberant young woman's cheek.

"You seem well-rested, Bash," Kayja observed. "Doesn't he, Miliya?"

"Yes, he does." She graced him with a warm smile. "How have you been?"

The man reached for her hand and planted a kiss on her fingers.

"Thank you, ladies. One week in Denver at my brother's hospitality changed me into the man you see, standing in front of you."

"To what do we owe the pleasure of your presence?" Kayja asked.

"I was headed to see Nakai and saw your buggy. Mama Louise said you walked over here, so I said to myself, 'Bash, here is a chance to be in the company of two beautiful women.'" Light sienna brown eyes flashed with merriment.

"Such a charmer," Miliya said, blushing.

"Since you're here, we're having a surprise dinner party for Nakai tomorrow, nothing too elaborate; family and close friends. Would you attend?"

His brows lifted. "Kayja, you do know he hates surprises?"

"Oh, sure. So what?" she laughed, winking at Miliya.

"You are a brave lady!" Bash grinned. "Where and what time?"

Turning to the woman standing next to her, she asked, "What do you think, Miliya?"

A frown creased her brow. "Let's have it here at the Estate Hall. This way, when he's expressing his dislike, I won't have far to hide." Slanted azure eyes glittered with amusement.

"That may be two of us," Kayja laughed. "Is seven a good time?"

"Yes," Miliya and Bash answered unanimously.

A loud knock made them whirl around to face the door.

"Expecting company, Miliya?" Bash asked.

"No." She frowned.

"Then let me do the honors," he offered.

"Who said chivalry is dead?" Miliya winked at Kayja.

Bash's long-legged stride moved to the door and swung it open.

Nakai stood rigid; his daunting eyes scanned him from head to toe.

"Bash." He nodded in greeting." Why are you here?"

"Oh, you offend my feelings!" Bash feigned pain. "I've been away a week, and this is all you can say to your friend?"

"Nakai!" Kayja said, excited, stepping around Bash.

Seeing his cousin, he hugged her.

"It's good to see you, Kay. Where is your hostess?" Nakai asked.

"Hi." Hearing his voice, Miliya responded. Why was he here? Most of the week, Nakai had attended meetings with prospective buyers, eating his meals in town with his associates. His absence was her

loss. Nakai crossed the room to where she stood, his eyes never left her face.

"Hello, Miliya." His voice is deep and mellow. "I missed you."

"You did?" Her voice was but a whisper.

"Ahem."

The pair turned, unaware of the two people in the room. Bash was whistling, his eyes darting about the room, his hands in his pants pockets. Kayja steered him out into the foyer.

"What's wrong with those two?" Nakai asked. He returned his stare to the starry-eyed woman gazing up at him. "Can't a man tell the woman he loves he missed her?"

She blinked at him in surprise. Her eyes raked over his handsome face and softened.

"This week, I've been through a wealth of emotions concerning you, and I finally understand one thing."

"Which is?"

He leaned a little closer. "I want to walk by your side through this lifetime and beyond. My passion for you is binding, final."

Their eyes met and held for a few moments. "My prayer is to be the man you need. I've been waiting for you to tell me how you felt about our relationship with no coercion from me." From his pants pocket. he pulled out a black velvet box and opened the lid. A gold. two carat diamond marquise bordered by diamond baguettes on either side, shone brilliantly.

"I bought this gem when I was in Butte a few weeks back." Nakai bent down on one knee, looking up at her, he asked, "Will you marry me?"

"Yes, I love you," Miliya said, wiping at the tears of joy rolling down her face. He rose and placed the ring on her finger.

Smiling, he pulled her into a bear hug. He was thankful Kayja, and Bash was in the foyer, or else this overwhelming feeling rushing through his body may have caused him a repentance prayer. The slow release of his embrace left her deprived of his warmth.

"I will speak to Falcon later. I have a feeling he won't be surprised."

"We're going to have a wedding!" Kayja ran into the room and hugged the pair. Bash gave the bride-to-be a peck on her cheek, then turned to his longtime friend and gave him a congratulatory pat on the back.

"You two deserve to be together after all the woes you've been through."

"Thanks, Bash. God, in His infinite mercy, has given me the woman I love unconditionally for eternity." Bash grinned. "A dream came to Pinesdale!"

EPILOGUE

Falcon sat up in bed, thinking about this evening's celebration.

The surprise birthday for Nakai was a jubilant affair. When he announced the engagement between Nakai and Miliya an uproar of cheers and applause had filled the room, along with tears of happiness.

Falcon couldn't ask for a better man for his sister than Nakai. Through all the trials and quandaries thrown in their path, the love and faith they shared grew strong and indestructible.

 Two months from now, the oldest Kensington brother will be the first to marry. The question going around is who is the next brother to follow his lead? Falcon knew he and his brothers didn't have any intentions to submit to the bonds of holy matrimony anytime soon.

He slid under the covers. To think a year ago, he didn't have a biological family, and today God has enriched his life with an estranged sister with whom he shared an eternal love. One day she would add to the Kensington lineage from her union with Nakai.

God's plan is like a fragrant rosebud; sweet and always blooming in his life. Falcon settled on his pillows; he would be a brother-in-law to his brother.

Two months later

"Miliya Marie Kensington," Nakai spoke into his wife's ear as he stood behind her posing for a photograph.

"Behave, my husband, and smile," she said in a hushed voice.

The photographer signaled he was finished, and the couple relaxed.

"Nemehotatse. I love you," he whispered in her ear.

She had floated down the aisle like an angelic being in the designer, white creation. The bridal party had comprised of Soma, as a bridesmaid, Kayja, maid of honor, and the three brothers as groomsmen. Falcon was the best man.

Joining the couple Kayja said, "I overheard someone say this wedding was a magnificent event. There are over ninety people here this evening. Thank goodness the Estate Hall has a capacity for a hundred. Nakai and I thank you so much Kayja for your expertise and your time."

"Anything for my two favorite people."

"Time? Did someone say time?" A masculine voice asked.

Lucas stepped up behind Kayja grinning, "It's time for you to dance with your husband since you have time to spare now." He wiggled his thick eyebrows.

Kayja speared him in the ribs. "Let's go, big boy!" The two dissolved into the crowd of dancers.

"Dance with me, Mrs. Kensington." Nakai took her hand and led her onto the floor.

"Did I tell you I love you?" Miliya stood on her toes and whispered in his ear.

"My heart belongs to you." His arm tightened around her waist. Dark eyes glanced around the room and lingered on a couple sitting and talking at a table huddled together.

"Is that Royce and Soma at that table over there?" Nakai pointed with his chin toward the young people.

Miliya smiled. She had noticed the young woman eyeing Royce on several occasions. How surprised Soma would be to know he returned the looks.

"I think my brother is smitten with Soma."

"I'll be watching to see how this friendship unfolds." Miliya said, and rested her head on her husband's chest. The ballad swirled around the newlyweds as they embraced each other, unaware the music had stopped.

"Hey, you two, the dance has ended," grinning, Dakota, and Falcon walked past them. The groom responded with a wink, took his bride's hand, slipped out of the banquet hall, and upstairs to the master bedroom.

"Nakai, our guests will wonder where we are," Miliya said, her heart pounding with anticipation.

"I don't believe so," he stated, removing his jacket. "This is our wedding night." Nakai pulled his wife into his arms and kissed her lips; any thoughts of the guests were forgotten.

www.ingramcontent.com/pod-product-compliance
Lightning Source LLC
Chambersburg PA
CBHW050359030726
47503CB00006B/1939